THE ASSASSINATION GAME

THE ASSASSINATION GAME

by Alan Gratz

Simon Spotlight
New York London Toronto Sydney New Delhi

This book is a work of fiction. Any references to historical events, real people, or real locales are used fictitiously. Other names, characters, places, and incidents are the product of the author's imagination, and any resemblance to actual events or locales or persons, living or dead, is entirely coincidental. SIMON SPOTLIGHT An imprint of Simon & Schuster Children's Publishing Division 1230 Avenue of the Americas, New York, New York 10020 © 2012 Paramount Pictures Corporation. ® & © 2012 CBS Studios, Inc. STAR TREK and related marks are trademarks of CBS Studios Inc. All Rights Reserved. All rights reserved, including the right of reproduction in whole or in part in any form. SIMON SPOTLIGHT and colophon are registered trademarks of Simon & Schuster, Inc. For information about special discounts for bulk purchases, please contact Simon & Schuster Special Sales at 1-866-506-1949 or business@simonandschuster.com. Manufactured in the United States of America 0612 FFG First Edition 10 9 8 7 6 5 4 3 2 1 ISBN 978-1-4424-2059-5 (hc) • ISBN 978-1-4424-2058-8 (pbk) • ISBN 978-1-4424-2060-1 (eBook) • Library of Congress Control Number: 2012934033

For my friends and colleagues on the USS *Potemkin*

THE ASSASSINATION GAME

Contents

CH.01.30
TAG

"Ladies, gentlemen, hermaphrodites, cogenitors, and asexual life-forms," Nadja Luther said, her eyes sweeping the Starfleet Academy cadets gathered around her, "welcome to the Assassination Game."

Leonard McCoy rolled his eyes as Jim Kirk grinned and nudged him.

"I don't know why I let you talk me into this nonsense," McCoy groused.

"You know *exactly* why, Bones, and if you don't be quiet, she's going to think you're not interested."

Jim was right. The only reason he'd come along for this damn fool business was because of the senior cadet leaning against a desk at the front of the classroom. Nadja Luther. She was lean, tall, and as cool as a mint julep in July. Her auburn hair reminded McCoy of a Mississippi sunset, and her blue eyes reminded him of Romulan ale. Perhaps most importantly, *nothing* about her reminded him of his ex-wife.

"The Assassination Game is simple," Nadja told them. "Each of you will be given the name of another player. Track down and assassinate that player. When you score a kill, you inherit your victim's target. If *you* are killed, you're out. The game ends when only one player remains."

The cadets around the room broke into quiet but animated discussions.

Kirk clapped his hands and wrung them like a supervillain in an old holo-novel. "This is going to be *great*."

"There are only two rules," Nadja went on, her easy voice bringing them all back to order. "One: You can only score a kill when you are alone with your victim. If there are any witnesses, whether they're players or not, there is no kill."

"Great, just great," McCoy said as the cadets in the room talked excitedly among themselves again. "Just what we all need—a little more paranoia in our lives."

Kirk smiled. "Just think, Bones—this is the perfect opportunity for you to get Cadet Luther alone."

"Yeah. If I can catch her."

"Rule two: The only weapon that counts for a kill is *this*," Nadja said, and she held up one standard-issue titanium Starfleet Academy cafeteria spork.

Those cadets whose species had a sense of humor laughed, and Nadja placed a tray of sporks onto the desk beside her.

"Do I have a volunteer to help me pass them out?" she asked sweetly.

McCoy felt a hand push him off the computer console upon which he sat, and he stumbled forward. He turned to glare at Kirk, but his friend was, at present, innocently examining his fingernails. McCoy cleared his throat, tugged at the bottom of his tunic, and tried to regain what little cool he previously possessed. Nadja smiled and put the tray of sporks in his hands.

"It's . . . Bones, isn't it?" she asked him.

"Leonard," he told her. "Leonard McCoy. But you can, um . . . you can call me Bones if you want to. My friends call me that. If you wanted to be my friend, I mean."

Nadja raised an eyebrow and grinned at him, and McCoy turned away, cursing himself. *Smooth, Leonard. Very smooth.* He shot a look at Kirk. Jim had his eyes closed and was shaking his head.

McCoy soldiered on, handing out sporks. There were at least two dozen cadets playing the game, including Humans, Saurians, Deltans, Tellarites, Efrosians, Andorians, one enormous Orion, and a catlike Caitian who purred as he took a spork. McCoy had just begun to calculate the odds that he would make it out of the room alive when there was a stir over by the windows.

"The Varkolak!" someone said, and within moments every cadet had warped to the other side of the room.

McCoy hurried over himself, unable to resist curiosity. It was hard to see well from this high up in the math and sciences building, but he could just glimpse a mob of leather and metal and fur—*lots* of fur—in between the battalion of Starfleet Security personnel who escorted the visitors to the empty barracks building where they would be staying. It was the first time McCoy had ever seen a Varkolak outside of holo-vids and medical journals, most of which were acknowledged to be inaccurate at best and wholly misleading at worst. He and the rest of Starfleet Medical hoped the upcoming Interspecies Medical Summit the Varkolak were there to attend would clear up some of the confusion.

"I've heard they bite the heads off live animals and drink their blood," whispered a cadet.

"My uncle says Varkolak howl at the moon," said another.

"You know how you get a promotion on a Varkolak ship? You kill the officer ahead of you."

"Professor Entarra says they're really here because they want Theta Cygni," bellowed Braxim, the big Xannon cadet who had become McCoy and Kirk's friend.

"Yeah, well, the Federation wants the Gavaria Sector, and I don't think the Varkolak are going to be giving that up soon," said another cadet.

"We have met the enemy, and it is them," Kirk said quietly.

"I don't think that's exactly how the expression goes," McCoy told him. Down below, the Varkolak contingency and their escorts disappeared into the barracks. "Show's over," McCoy announced.

"Yeah," Kirk said. "And can we wrap this up? I'm actually supposed to be down there on Added Security Detail at 1300 hours."

McCoy finished handing out the sporks, and Nadja jangled a black felt bag that focused them all on her again.

"Each of you has given me a spare Academy badge with your name and serial number on it. Those badges are here in this bag. When I come around, you'll each draw one. The name you draw is your first target. If you draw your own name, drop the badge back into the bag and draw again."

McCoy tried not to stare at Nadja Luther as she started around the room, holding the bag out to each player as he, she, or it drew a name. *Why her?* McCoy asked himself. Why had Nadja suddenly become the object of his affections? She was mature, yes. As a senior she was at least close to his relatively advanced age, a result of his having attended eight years of medical school before joining the Academy. She had a take-charge, no-nonsense attitude he loved too. She was one of those people—like Jim Kirk—who you knew was going to be a captain someday. Someday soon. And then, of course, there was her smile, which lit up her face and sent shivers running down McCoy's spine.

Nadja stepped in front of him, and he blushed like she could read his mind. It was his strong suspicion, based on years of experience but no hard scientific evidence, that women were, secretly, telepathic. At least the girls he'd dated had been. He tried to smile as Nadja offered him the bag, but he suspected it came out more like a grimace.

McCoy cleared his throat, pulled a badge from the bag, and barely glanced at it long enough to see that it wasn't his. McCoy hardly cared about the game, the Varkolak, his upcoming xenobiology exam, or *anything*, for that matter, that was not named Nadja Luther. Nadja smiled at him and moved on to Kirk, leaving the scent of lavender and apple blossoms in her wake.

Probably just her damn shampoo, McCoy groused to himself. *Forget a cure for the common cold. What we really need is a vaccine for falling in love.*

Beside him, Kirk pulled out a badge, read the name, flipped it into the air, and caught it confidently. Nadja moved on, and soon she was back in front of the room, where she put her own hand inside the bag and drew the last of the badges. She looked at the name, smiled, and slid it into her pocket. McCoy found himself hoping she'd pulled *his* name from the bag, and realized probably half the cadets in the room were thinking the same thing.

"That's it," Nadja told the cadets. "You have your targets. There are no safety zones and no time-outs. The Assassination Game begins *now*."

The cadets in the room eyed one another warily and began to leave in groups of three and four. McCoy was about to suggest that he and Kirk leave with Braxim when his friend's eyes told him something else was up. He turned to find Nadja coming their way.

"I was thinking, Leonard McCoy," she said, "that I would like to be able to call you Bones. But as I understand it, that name is reserved for friends."

She was smiling coyly, but McCoy still went red at the reminder of his earlier flub.

"I was wondering," she went on, "what a girl has to do to become . . . your friend?"

McCoy observed almost intuitively that he was exhibiting symptoms of dyspnea and tachycardia, which he diagnosed as shortness of breath and an increased heart rate due to exposure to an actual potential date. He swallowed and tried to take a deep breath.

"Well, a friendly drink together at the Warp Core around 2100 hours would be a good start," he told her.

"The Warp Core at 2100 hours then . . . Leonard," Nadja said, and she left with the last group of cadets.

"That's what I'm talking about!" Kirk said, clapping him on the shoulder. "She's interested in you, Bones."

"Either that or she's just trying to get me alone to kill me."

"Oh, I don't think it's that," Kirk told him.

"Why not?"

McCoy felt something poke him in the ribs, and he looked down to see Kirk sticking him with the business end of a standard-issue titanium Starfleet Academy cafeteria spork. In his other hand, Kirk waggled a golden Starfleet Academy badge with McCoy's name and serial number engraved on the back.

Kirk grinned apologetically. "Tag."

"Jim," McCoy told him, "sometimes you're a real bastard."

CH.02.30
How to Speak Varkolak

Kirk barreled down the corridor and turned the corner so fast, he had to slam on the brakes so as not to run right into the Starfleet Security officer addressing a group of Academy cadets. A group of Academy cadets Kirk was supposed to be a part of.

"Oh, nice of you to join us, Mr."—The officer consulted his PADD—"Kirk, is it?"

Kirk nodded, too out of breath to say more. "I was—I was—"

I was really stupid not to have thought up a good excuse while I was sprinting over here.

"I, uh, I heard Cadet Kirk called away to deliver a message to Admiral Barnett just a few minutes ago," another cadet piped up. It was a man named Leslie, whom Kirk recognized from his Elementary Temporal Mechanics class. Kirk nodded his thanks and made a note to buy Leslie a drink sometime.

The officer got in Leslie's face. "Funny how you failed to mention that when I called role, Mr. Leslie."

"Sorry, sir. It won't happen again, sir," Kirk said.

The officer turned on him with fire in his eyes, and Kirk knew immediately he'd made a mistake. Behind the officer, Leslie winced.

"'Sir'? *'Sir'?* Do you see any stripes on my sleeve, Cadet?"

Kirk kicked himself. There *weren't* any stripes on the man's sleeve, which, of course, meant he was either Starfleet's oldest living ensign or he was a noncommissioned officer, a regular enlistee who never went through the Academy. Only commissioned officers got the "sir" treatment, and noncoms hated it when you screwed up and called them "sir." Once Kirk and the rest of the cadets made ensign, they would technically rank higher than any noncom, no matter how long the noncom had served, but you still showed proper respect for enlisted officers if you knew what was good for you.

"No, Chief," Kirk said.

"That's right, Cadet. Because I *work* for a living. Now fall in."

Kirk hurriedly took a place at the back, sharing a quick glance of thanks and commiseration with Leslie.

"All right. *As I was saying*, Cadets," the chief continued, a scowl still on his face. "You are hereby assigned to a special Added Security Detail under my command for as long as the Varkolak are with us. Individually, you will be assigned shifts and posts throughout the barracks and public spaces our foul-smelling visitors are permitted to go. Now, you may not have noticed, Cadets, but Starfleet happens to already have quite a few security officers. Well-trained, *experienced* security officers. We do not *need* a special Added Security Detail. But Admiral Barnett thinks it's a good idea for some of his cadets to get up close and personal with these animals, seeing as you're supposed to be the *future* of Starfleet." The disdain in the chief's voice told them just what he thought about Starfleet's prospects if the cadets in front of him were its future. "But understand, Cadets: You are not to talk to the Varkolak. You are not to make eye contact with the Varkolak. You are not so much as to *breathe* in a Varkolak's general direction. If a real security situation arises, *real* Starfleet Security will take care of it. Your one and only job is to be furniture."

Kirk rolled his eyes for Leslie's benefit. This chief was a real piece of work.

"Do I make myself clear?" the chief barked.

"Yes, Chief!" the cadets said as one.

The chief read out their posts, and Kirk and Leslie hurried off to their first assignment: the conference room. The room was windowless and spartan but for a large oval table surrounded by ten chairs. With a sinking feeling, Kirk realized there was no guarantee the room would be used at all during their three-hour shift.

"So," Kirk said, "which corner do you like? The empty one with no window view or the empty one with no window view?"

Leslie laughed and took a corner opposite Kirk.

"Thanks for having my back back there," Kirk told him. "I owe you."

"No problem," Leslie told him. "You can return the favor by bringing me on as a crewman when you get your command."

Kirk laughed. "What makes you think they're going to give me a ship?"

"They'd be crazy not to."

Kirk smiled. He liked the reputation he was getting at the Academy.

"You think we should just sit down at the table? Put our feet up?" he asked Leslie. "I have a feeling we're going to be staring at each other for three hours."

"We'd better play it straight," Leslie told him. "You never know when Chief Hard Ass is going to come checking on us."

"All right. The chief said our one and only job was to be furniture, so I'm just going to stand here and pretend I'm a three-dimensional chess set."

"I think that may qualify as more of a game than a

piece of furniture," Leslie said.

"Yeah. Just to be safe then, I'll be a lamp instead."

Leslie chuckled, and they settled in for what promised to be a long haul. At least Leslie wasn't in the Assassination Game, so Kirk didn't have to worry about him sticking a spork in him while no one was watching. With nothing better to do, Kirk put a hand in his pants pocket and fingered the two Academy badges there: Bones's and the one he'd taken off of Bones when he "killed" him. It belonged to the big Orion, Ard Jarikar. *That* was going to be a challenge. Then again, Orions were known for their arrogance, and Ard Jarikar was no exception. He probably wouldn't be as careful as some of the other players. And it wasn't like Kirk was going to actually have to *fight* him. Maybe he could catch him on the way back to the dorm after a Parrises Square match, when Ard Jarikar was tired and distracted. . . .

The door opened, and Kirk and Leslie snapped to attention. It proved to be just a Starfleet science team entering the room, but they wheeled in a desk-sized computer console with them, which was promising. What was even more promising was the arrival of one of Kirk's favorite cadets.

"Uhura! Hey."

Cadet Uhura, looking amazing and meticulously put together as usual, didn't bother looking up from her PADD.

"Come on, Uhura," Kirk said. "I know you're busy, but you can at least say hello."

Uhura continued to ignore Kirk, like she couldn't hear him, which he knew was impossible. As the Academy's foremost xenolinguistics student, she had the best ears on campus. And those ears were connected to a face that wasn't too bad to look at, in Kirk's opinion.

"I can't even get a 'Hey, Jim'?" he pleaded.

One of the noncadet scientists with Uhura, an Andorian man, glanced back and forth between Kirk and Uhura, clearly wondering why the cadet wasn't responding, but afraid to ask.

"All right," Kirk said. "If you don't talk to me, I'm just going to tell embarrassing stories about you in front of all your scientist friends. Like that one time at that bar called the Delta Quadrant when you drank six—"

Uhura was in his face in seconds. "I'm *working*, Kirk," she whispered. "Maybe you've heard of it?"

Kirk smiled. "I'm working too," he told her.

"Doing what?"

"I'm being a lamp."

The conference room door opened again, and this time three Varkolak came in, surrounded by Starfleet Security officers. Kirk and Uhura turned and stared. It was the first time Kirk had seen Varkolak up close, and they were just as ugly as promised. And as malodorous. Kirk could smell them from across the room—a musty, animal smell like . . . well, like dogs, which is what they most resembled. Or perhaps, with their long snouts, pointed ears, long and bushy tails, and sharp teeth, they were best described as bipedal wolves. *Werewolves*, Kirk thought with an inward shudder.

The important one of the three, the one who stopped when he entered the room and licked his jagged teeth like a hungry sehlat, was tall and broad-shouldered. Most of his fur was a blend of black, brown, gray, and white, but unlike the others, he had a patch of white fur, like a collar around his neck. He sniffed the air as he came in, and his animal-like eyes swept the room.

What big eyes you have, Grandmother, Kirk thought.

Those wolf eyes found Kirk and Uhura staring at him, and Uhura hurried back to her place with the rest of the scientists while Kirk came to attention again.

"Dr. Lartal," said one of the Federation scientists, "thank you for joining us. Won't you sit down?"

The Varkolak snarled at the greeting for some reason, and Kirk could already tell he was going to dislike this man. Lartal sat with an arrogant casualness while the other two Varkolak stood behind him.

"We know you're here for the medical conference," the scientist said, "but those of us in the linguistics department couldn't resist the opportunity to enhance the Varkolak database in our universal translator." She nodded to the console they had wheeled in, operated by the Andorian scientist. "Varkolak has proven particu-larly difficult for our linguistics algorithms."

"Of course," Lartal told her. His voice was a low growl. "Varkolak is an incredibly complex language using a combi-nation of words, smells, and body movements. Many adult Varkolak have only a rudimentary knowledge of it them-selves. The idea that some *bRuah grrRok* could learn it is ludi-crous." As he spoke the Varkolak words, he rolled his head and squirmed in his seat.

"Oh, this is good, this is good," the scientist said, motion-ing to the Andorian. "Make sure you have it running." She turned back to Lartal. "Could you count to twenty for us?"

Lartal growled, then lazily recited, *"Raat, ri, hiRu, gau, bRost, zei, zapzi, gRol, uRezni, rezni, rezni Raat, rezni ri, rezni hiRu—* Bah! This is a waste of time."

"Oh, no, no!" the scientist told him. "Perhaps if you could give us some common Varkolak phrases."

"Gizon bRat nabaRmentza guten aRte haize Bere harrRa-pariak harrRapari bihuRtza da," Lartal said, moving in his chair. The other two Varkolak chuckled.

"'Wind above . . . with a man who stands out from its prey . . . becomes predator'?" the Andorian read off the computer screen.

"No, no, no," Lartal growled. "'The man who stands upwind from his prey becomes the prey.' You see? This is pointless."

"If you would just bear with us a little longer," the lead scientist said. "Just say anything that comes to mind."

Lartal scowled at her. *"ZuRe sugurrR hezea ga,"* he said. "'Your nose is wet.'" The two Varkolak goons behind him laughed again, but the scientist didn't seem to mind. She was more interested in the words. Leslie was looking angry, though, and Kirk shook his head at him to remind him they weren't supposed to get involved.

"ZuRe ama katu gat izan zan, aR zuRe aita baRa txarrRak ArdoaRen usaina!" Lartal said, and his companions roared with laughter again.

"'Your mother, she was a kitten, and your father, he smelled of berry wine?'" the Andorian read off the screen to more howls from the Varkolak. Lartal banged a paw on the table, tears in his eyes.

Across the room, Leslie balled his fists and took a step away from the wall.

"Don't do it, Leslie," Kirk called. "They're not worth it."

Lartal looked up at Kirk, then behind him at Leslie, who was standing his ground. Lartal's eyes got wider, if that was possible, and he smiled a great fanged smile.

"ZakuR ona!" he said, rising from his seat. "So perhaps not all of you are simpering *kumea*. Are there men of teeth among you, then?" He stepped up close to Leslie. "Or are they all like your admiral Barnett? Soft and shapeless, like a Regulan blood worm?"

Leslie rocked forward, and Kirk could tell he was itching to fight. "Take it easy, Leslie," Kirk told him. "Everyone's entitled to an opinion."

"That's right," Lartal said, still face-to-face with Leslie. "And if I think that Barnett is a Denebian slime devil, well, that's my opinion too, isn't it?"

Leslie swelled up, trying to match the Varkolak's size, and the Starfleet Security officers in the room put their hands to their phasers. The two Varkolak with Lartal did too.

"Don't do it, Leslie," Kirk called. "We have our orders." Leslie had his back with the chief, and Kirk was ready to return the favor, but he wasn't anxious to do it going toe-to-toe with some of the galaxy's most notorious fighters. "Just forget it. It's not worth fighting for. We're big enough to take a few insults."

Leslie nodded and relaxed, focusing his eyes at the wall across the room again.

"Bah! Are there no men here whose blood boils with the spirit of the hunt? The call of the wild?" Lartal asked.

"Not today, Lartal," Kirk said, more for Leslie's benefit than the Varkolak's. The Varkolak came around to him and stood so close that Kirk could smell what he'd had for lunch—and still see some of it in his teeth.

"And has nobody ever told you, Cadet, that prey never chooses its day to die?"

"Who says I'm going to roll over and play dead?" Kirk said.

Another ugly smile opened like a gash on the Varkolak's face.

"And how, Dr., would you translate *'Bat histari ona ga hobia hamar in gaina ga'?"* the lead scientist asked, oblivious to the challenge on Kirk's and Lartal's faces.

The Varkolak closed his eyes in exasperation.

"Bat ehiztarrRi ona ga hobea hamaR engaina ga," he said, barking the syllables. "You cannot speak Varkolak because you do not speak with *gRina . . . momarrRa.* What is the word?"

"Wildness," Uhura said. "Ferocity."

"Yes," Lartal said.

"Hortza aR atzaparrR ziren Varkolak graio zan," Uhura said, in what Kirk thought was a perfect imitation of the Varkolak growling and squirming. Lartal must have thought so too, for his eyes lit up. Even Lartal's bodyguards looked impressed.

"'From tooth and claw were the Varkolak born,'" Uhura translated for the rest of them.

"Yes," Lartal said. He strode over to Uhura, leering at her. "Now here is an Earth woman worthy of a Varkolak warrior. A bit less . . . *ample* than a Varkolak woman, perhaps. Hairless and thin, like a shaven *katu,* but that would just make her easier to mount."

The other Varkolak laughed, and Uhura flushed and stared at her PADD.

Kirk cleared his throat. "Perhaps you'd like to rephrase that, Dr.? I think something might have been lost in the translation."

Lartal grinned again and crossed to Kirk. "You're right. I should. I didn't mean to say she would be easy to mount. What I meant to say was, I would take this Earth woman into my bed and make her my bitch."

"That's what I thought you meant," Kirk said, and he reared back and slugged the Varkolak.

CH.03.30
The Invitation

"I want to know who started it."

Admiral Barnett stared down the line of Starfleet Security officers and cadets, all of whom were battered and bruised—including Uhura, who had jumped into the fray as soon as the conference room turned into a bar fight. Kirk had seen her deliver a kick to Lartal that was going to leave him limping for a week.

"I'm waiting," Barnett said, but no one spoke up.

The admiral stopped in front of one of the Starfleet Security officers. "Lieutenant Freeman, who started the fight?"

Kirk knew what was coming. The officers would sell him out, blame it on the cadets.

"I don't know, sir," the lieutenant said.

Kirk breathed a sigh of relief. Maybe Lartal was right after all. Maybe there *were* men of "teeth" in Starfleet. Or at least men ready to defend a woman's honor.

Barnett gave Freeman a look that told him just how much he believed him, and moved on.

"Cadet Uhura," he said. "You're one of the Academy's finest students. I can't believe you would let yourself get dragged into this. Tell me who started it."

Uhura stood rigid. "I don't know, sir."

"'I don't know, sir,'" Barnett repeated. "I want to know who threw the first punch, people." No one spoke up. His eyes shifted to Kirk and lingered there for a moment, and Kirk was afraid the admiral was going to ask him point-blank if he'd thrown the first punch. Would he be able to lie to him?

"All right," Barnett said at last. "Officers will receive an official reprimand and cadets will be restricted to their dormitories when not in class until I find out who started it. Dismissed."

The cadets and officers turned and hurried out of Barnett's office, but the admiral held back Kirk.

"Not you, Kirk."

Out of the corner of his eye, Kirk saw Uhura turn and give him a look that was a cross between frustration and sympathy before the door to Barnett's office slid closed.

The admiral left Kirk standing where he was and picked up a PADD from his desk.

"James Tiberius Kirk," Admiral Barnett read. "Disciplinary record."

Kirk's heart sank.

"I see here, Mr. Kirk, that you have been involved in no less than *nine* fights in your short time at the Academy."

"That's nine *including* . . . this one . . . sir," Kirk said, trailing off as Barnett's face told him that he was not helping his cause. The admiral laid the PADD on his desk and folded his arms.

"Mr. Kirk, I absolutely refuse to believe you were just in the right room at the wrong time. Are you really going to let all those good men and women take a phaser for you on this one?"

Kirk looked at his boots. Admitting what he'd done might be his proverbial last straw at the Academy and see him sent packing, and the others had made it clear they were willing to take an official reprimand to protect him. But keeping quiet wasn't right, and he knew it.

"No, sir."

"Who threw the first punch?"

"I did, Admiral."

"Cadet Kirk, what in the name of Zefram Cochrane possessed you to start a fistfight with a group of Varkolak doctors in the middle of one of the most difficult and tenuous periods in the history of Varkolak–Federation relations?"

"About that, sir. I don't think Lartal is really a doctor. He just—"

"Cadet Kirk! I asked you a question."

"He insulted us, sir."

"It must have been some insult!"

"It was, sir. Cadet Leslie wanted to have a go at him, but I told him not to."

"You . . . told Leslie *not* to start a fight. And why did Mr. Leslie want to start a fight with the Varkolak?"

"Is this off the record, sir?"

"No, it's not off the record!"

Kirk swallowed. "Because . . . the Varkolak called you soft and shapeless . . . like a Regulan blood worm."

"Ah," Admiral Barnett said. Clearly he hadn't expected the insults to be about him. "Is that all?"

"No, sir. They also compared you to a Denebian slime devil."

"I get the picture," the admiral said, cutting him off. "So after they said all this, that's when you hit the Varkolak?"

"Oh no, sir."

Admiral Barnett blanched. "No?"

"No, sir. The chief, he told us not to make trouble, and I didn't see that it was worth fighting about. After all, we're big enough to take a few insults, aren't we?"

Admiral Barnett cleared his throat. "And what exactly was it they said that started the fight, then?"

"Lartal made some indecent remarks to Cadet Uhura."

"Cadet . . . Uhura," the admiral said.

"Yes, sir."

"You started a fight with the Federation's most notorious enemies because they insulted Cadet Uhura, not because they—"

"I couldn't just let them insult a woman like that, Admiral!"

The admiral sighed. "No. Of course not." Barnett went behind his desk to sit down, and Kirk waited for the other shoe to drop. *Whatever comes, comes*, he thought. *I can always get a job as a freighter captain. Or a bouncer.*

"That little stunt of yours has had repercussions, Mr. Kirk. Do you understand that?"

"Yes, sir."

"I don't think you do. For the duration of the Varkolak's stay, Mr. Kirk, you are hereby assigned to be the personal liaison for Dr. Lartal when you're not in class or otherwise engaged in required Academy activities."

"I— *What?*" Kirk stammered, hastily adding a "sir."

"It seems you've won an admirer," Admiral Barnett told him. "Dr. Lartal came to me and asked for you specifically. He also asked that you not be disciplined for your behavior. He told me two weeks in space is too long for a Varkolak to go without a good fight, and you were . . . just what the doctor ordered."

Kirk couldn't believe his good luck, and he smiled.

"Don't get the wrong idea here, Cadet," the admiral told

him. "This is a highly charged situation. Do I need to remind you of the lives the Federation lost to the Varkolak at the battle of Vega V? The slightest misstep while these Varkolak are here could touch off a war between the Varkolak Assembly and the Federation, and no one wants that. Which means I had better not find out there's been a fight number *ten*, Mr. Kirk. Dismissed."

Uhura read the strange message on her PADD again: CADET NYOTA UHURA, PLEASE COME ALONE TO ROOM 1033, SHRAN HALL, TONIGHT AT 2300 HOURS. The invitation was signed only with a tiny logo of an atom. She checked the time and the number on the door again and then stepped inside. It was dark in the classroom, and the lights didn't come on automatically as they were supposed to when she walked in. Uhura stayed close to the door, so it would remain open while she found the manual light switch on the wall, but a voice in the darkness made her jump.

"It's all right, Cadet Uhura. We prefer the lights stay off." In the darkness, first one, then another, and then a host of flashlights clicked on, illuminating an empty area in the middle of the room. Uhura stepped toward the light, and the door slid shut behind her.

"Who are you? What is this?" Uhura asked.

"We are the Graviton Society," the same male voice

told her. He swept his flashlight beam up at his face, but everything above his mouth was shrouded by the cowl of a dark cloak. The others did the same, and Uhura saw she was in a room full of cloaked people.

The Graviton Society. Uhura had heard whispers about it since she was a first-year cadet. Everybody talked about it, but no one knew exactly what it was—or if it really existed.

"What is this, some kind of secret club?" she asked.

"We certainly do wish to remain . . . out of sensor range," the voice said. The pitch, the tone, the modulation—she could almost place whose voice it was. . . .

"You're trying to figure out who I am from the sound of my voice," the speaker said. "And no, I'm not a telepath. We were told you would do that. I'm using a voice modulator to disguise who I am."

"Why do you need disguises?" Uhura asked.

"Because we do things we wish to remain secret and prefer our existence not to be known outside our circle. Very few of us even know who all our members are."

"Bad things?"

"Quite the contrary. Everything we do is for the benefit of the Federation."

"Like what? You hold bake sales?"

"Like the coup that splintered the Breen Confederacy before they attacked the Grazer home world. Or the cure for the Hruffa Bison plague that ended the forced Varkolak expansion and bought the Federation the current stalemate it enjoys. How do you think we've been able to avoid all-out war when humans and Varkolak can't be in the same room together for ten minutes without fighting?"

He had to mean what had happened in the conference room. But Uhura had come straight here from Admiral Barnett's office. How did they already know?

"You're telling me a bunch of cadets with flashlights brought down the Breen Confederacy?" Uhura said.

The mouth under the cowl smiled. "Not us, no. But once you're a Graviton, you're always a Graviton. As we graduate, we join the ranks of Starfleet, but our allegiance to the Graviton Society remains. After many years now, there are Gravitons in almost every branch of Starfleet."

Uhura's skin prickled. There was a certain cache that would come from being part of a fraternity with its roots deep in Starfleet, even if she couldn't talk about it. The possibility of inside information, preferential promotions, and a voice in guiding the direction of the organization, no matter what her rank or position. But the idea was a little frightening, too.

"Why?" Uhura asked. "Why does Starfleet need any special help? Why can't you work for Starfleet through official channels?"

"We do, and we will. But we believe Starfleet has become too complacent, Cadet Uhura, and so we are dedicated to doing the things it cannot do—or will not do—to protect it and guarantee its survival against extreme threats."

"And are we under extreme threat?" Uhura asked.

"Always, Cadet. I refer you, specifically, to the periorbital hematoma around your left eye."

Her black eye from the fight with the Varkolak. Uhura gingerly put a hand to it, and winced.

"Cadet Uhura, you have been identified as an outstanding student and a future leader within Starfleet. Will you join us?"

Flattery will get you everywhere, Uhura thought, and she found herself actually considering it. It was quite an invitation. But join a supersecret society that operated inside Starfleet yet *outside* its rules? A clandestine group who had as much as admitted to her that anything goes, as long as the ends justified the means?

"What if I refuse?" Uhura asked.

"We don't think you will. But if you choose not to join us, you will never hear from us—or about us—again."

"I—I need to think about it."

"Of course. But know, Cadet, that only the best of the best are asked to join the Graviton Society. Membership is by invitation only, and you come highly recommended."

"Oh, yes?" Uhura said. "Who recommended me?"

One of the hooded figures in the crowd stepped forward and flipped back his hood to reveal a familiar face.

A *very* familiar face.

"I did," said Spock.

CH.04.30
A Walk in the Park

"I know you're hiding in there, you little bastard. Now come out where I can see you."

Dr. Leonard McCoy adjusted a dial on the experimental analyzer he was using and checked the readings again. He was trying to find the proverbial needle in the haystack—a single molecule of boridium in a bowl of minestrone soup. He knew it was in there, because he'd put it in himself.

"No, no, no, no. Boridium, you bucket of bolts. Not beta-carotene. Come on."

It was late in the afternoon, and classes were long since over, but for Starfleet Academy cadets, the end of classes hardly meant the end of the school day. A number of McCoy's fellow medical students sat at workstations around the lab, like him, doing homework or working on independent research projects.

McCoy made a note of the previous attempt's settings on his PADD and recalibrated the machine. "Let's try this again, shall we?" McCoy told the analyzer.

"Do you always talk to your equipment?" a woman's voice asked.

McCoy looked up, a smart retort loaded into his hypospray for whomever couldn't mind their own business, and found himself staring at the very stare-worthy legs of Nadja Luther.

"I suppose the better question is, does it ever talk back?" she said.

"I—Nadja? How did you get in here?" McCoy asked. "I mean, hello."

Nadja smiled. "When you didn't hear me tapping on the glass, one of the others took pity on me and let me in."

"I'm sorry. I thought we were meeting at the bar."

"So did I. I've been waiting there for almost an hour. I have to say, Leonard, if you're playing hard to get, you're doing a good job."

McCoy blinked. "An hour?" He checked the clock on his PADD—it was still twenty minutes until 2100 hours. "We said 2100 hours."

Nadja shook her head. "You said 2000 hours."

McCoy could swear he'd said 2100 hours, not 2000 hours, but it didn't matter. What mattered was that the girl of his dreams (at least his recent ones) had sat waiting for him in a bar for forty minutes and had to come looking for him when he didn't show. He hastily shut down his equipment and cycled down his PADD.

"I'm so sorry," he said. "Let me make it up to you. There's still plenty of night left—"

Nadja put up a hand. "I've got to get back to my room and let Mrs. Penelope go to the bathroom."

"I'm guessing Mrs. Penelope isn't your roommate. At least I hope she isn't."

"Not my cadet roommate, no. I went right to the Warp Core from soccer practice, and I need to take my dog for a walk."

McCoy stood and offered Nadja his hand. "How about an escort, then?"

"Oh. How gallant. I accept."

McCoy led Nadja to the door of the lab. "McCoy, Leonard, Dr.," he told the voice-recognition program at the door. "Alpha seven, seven two delta epsilon." A light on the console blinked green, and the glass door slid open. The medical research lab wasn't exactly the Klingon prison planet of Rura Penthe when it came to security, but the voice-recognition passwords were enough to keep good people honest, as McCoy's grandfather used to say.

Nadja fished around for something in her purse and found it. She checked her lipstick in the reflection of her communicator and put it back.

"We good to go?" McCoy asked.

Nadja smiled. "Absolutely."

• · . ✦ · ✦ • ✦ · . •

James Kirk rubbed his eyes and leaned back on his lab stool. It was past 2100 hours. *Right now, I could be laying out under the stars with Cadet Areia*, Kirk thought. Cadet Areia, the *Deltan*. And a Deltan who hadn't yet taken the oath, for heaven's sake! They said a night with a Deltan was so mind-blowing, it could actually, *literally*, drive you insane.

Kirk was willing to risk it.

But this assignment to babysit the Varkolak was already putting a serious crimp in his social life, and it hadn't even officially started yet. Unless Kirk wanted to fail exochemistry, he had to get his lab work done *before* tomorrow's class, and to get his lab work done, he had to do it *tonight*, rather than the two-hour block he *used* to have free before class tomorrow. Which meant he'd had to call Areia and break off their date. Worse, she didn't believe him; she thought the only way he'd cancel on her was because he'd gotten a better offer, and she'd hung up in a huff.

"A *Deltan*," he lamented with a moan.

"Daydreaming again, Jimmy?"

Kirk snapped up straight. He knew that voice. He knew that voice all too well. Before him stood Jake Finnegan, an upperclassman who'd tormented him from the day Kirk had set foot on campus. He was bulky and silver-haired, with ruddy cheeks and a mean smile. Future redshirt material. He'd never known what he had done to draw his attention, although Kirk suspected he'd just happened to be the first plebe Finnegan had seen on that first day of school. From that point on, Kirk had been Jake Finnegan's personal project.

"Finnegan. What happened? You eat your handlers?"

Finnegan pulled a spork from his pocket and twirled it between his fingers. "Yeah," he said. "And now I'm ready for dessert."

A spork. *The Assassination Game*, Kirk realized with horror. Finnegan had pulled *his* badge from the black velvet bag? How unlucky was that?

Kirk scanned the room. It was empty! There had been at least three other cadets in here working when he'd come in, but he'd been so focused on his own work, he hadn't even noticed them leave.

Finnegan smiled and took a step closer.

Kirk stood quickly, knocking over the test tubes he'd been mixing chemicals in. Finnegan was around the lab bench in a heartbeat, bearing down on Kirk with the spork.

"Hold it, Finnegan! Seriously! Stop!" Kirk cried, his eyes on the spilled chemicals.

Finnegan paused, looking back and forth between Kirk and the lab bench. "What?"

"Don't . . . move," Kirk said. He held himself rigid and

stared wide-eyed at the lab bench. "Finnegan, do you have any idea what corbomite is?

"No."

That didn't surprise Kirk, as he'd just made it up.

"It's highly reactive," Kirk explained. "Just the slightest bump, the smallest vibration, can set it off. It takes the energy of whatever hits it and returns it a thousandfold. A millionfold. And I just . . . accidentally . . . made some."

Finnegan looked like he didn't want to believe Kirk, but he didn't know enough to be sure. Kirk kept his eyes on the grayish blob, even though Finnegan was close enough now he could have reached out and touched Kirk with the spork if he'd wanted to. The fact that Kirk was ignoring him completely and focusing on the "corbomite" helped sell it.

"Just this much could destroy everything within ten kilometers and leave a dead zone for four years," Kirk told him.

"What the hell are you doing making a bomb for?" Finnegan asked.

"I told you. It was an *accident*. You come barging in here while I'm working with chemicals and—"

The chemicals began to bubble and hiss.

"Get out! Get out!" Kirk cried. He dropped to the floor, his hands over his head, and watched from under the table as Finnegan bolted from the room.

Kirk stood quickly, swept the harmless mixture into

the sink, snatched up his PADD and his backpack, and ran for the door. He had to put as much distance as he could between him and Finnegan before the lunkhead realized there hadn't been a boom.

"A *Deltan*," Kirk muttered as he ran. "I could have been getting my mind blown by a Deltan. . . ."

"It's a phoretic analyzer," McCoy explained to Nadja as they walked along a trail in the Marin Headlands. A bright, glowing panorama of San Francisco at night was framed across the bay by the Golden Gate Bridge. "Dr. Huer developed it, and a few other cadets and I were invited to be a part of the laboratory trials. The idea is that it can take a complex mix of substances and identify individual molecules within it."

"A superscanner," Nadja said.

Nadja's dog, a little cairn terrier, stopped to sniff a bush.

"You could call it that. With a very specific medical use. Nothing like those scanners the Varkolak are supposed to have, of course. What I wouldn't give to get my hands on one of those."

The conversation lulled, and McCoy realized he'd been doing all the talking—a cardinal first-date sin.

"So. Enough about my boring research project," he said. "Tell me everything about yourself, beginning with your parents and your parents' parents and leading up to, oh, this afternoon."

Nadja laughed. "Well, my grandfather was German, and my grandmother was Russian. I'm named after her. After my parents met in college, they got the crazy idea to move to the Vega colony. I was born on the way."

"A space boomer, eh? That explains a lot."

"Does it?"

"Sure. Why else would anyone want to join up with an organization that ships you off into space on five-year missions, trapped inside a glorified tin can with a warp engine strapped to it?"

"That doesn't explain why *you* joined up, Leonard McCoy."

"Oh no. We're talking about you, remember? I think you left off around the time you were born, which means you've got another couple of decades to cover."

The path they were walking on came out into a large open area where tourists from around the quadrant were taking holo-pics of the San Francisco skyline. Mrs. Penelope barked at a squirrel and gave chase, and McCoy and Nadja sat on a bench.

"There's not much else to tell. I spent the early part of my life in the Vega colony, then my parents died, and I was shipped back to Earth to be raised by my grandparents in Frankfurt. I spent a couple of years in college, then applied for Starfleet Academy and got in. And here I am."

"Seems like there's an awful lot in there to tell," McCoy said. "I'm sorry about your parents."

Nadja shrugged. "It was a long time ago."

She left it at that, and so did McCoy.

Mrs. Penelope emerged from a copse a few meters away and ran toward a small group of people farther down the overlook, barking her head off.

"Uh-oh," Nadja said. "Looks like we have a distress call."

McCoy nodded. "Starfleet regulations mandate we check it out."

As they got closer, McCoy saw Mrs. Penelope harrying a group of protesters with signs. They chanted, "Varkolak, go home," over the little terrier's barking and held signs that read IF YOU'RE NOT WITH US, YOU'RE AGAINST US, and FEDERATION FIRST. The tourists were doing their best to avoid them, but the group had claimed one of the best photo-op spots on the headlands.

"What is this nonsense?" McCoy asked. Nadja picked up her dog and quieted her, but the protesters kept chanting without answering him. McCoy had little patience for close-minded, xenophobic attitudes like this, though he knew they still existed on Earth. Not all the protesters were human, though, including, he was angry to realize, a Tellarite medical cadet he knew from the Academy. He got in the cadet's face.

"You. Your name's Daagen, isn't it? You're a Starfleet cadet, man! You joined an organization dedicated to openness. Peaceful exploration. Diplomacy. 'Varkolak, go home'? 'Federation First'? You can't have it both ways."

The short, bearded, snout-faced Tellarite smiled. "You forget, Dr. McCoy—it is McCoy, isn't it? You forget, Dr., that the Federation began as a defensive alliance. A shield raised against our common enemies. So I *can* have it both ways. I can at once be dedicated to the organization I chose to serve and insist that its enemies—who do not share its lofty ideals, I might note—not be allowed to wander the grounds of its headquarters."

"Damn it, man, we're not going to bring peace to the galaxy by alienating everyone who doesn't agree with us. We've got to find common ground, and that starts by talking. Getting rid of some of the mystery. The misconceptions and misunderstandings. We show 'em enough of who we are, and maybe one day the Varkolak will join us."

"Next you would have me believe we will one day be allies with the Klingons," Daagen said.

Behind Daagen, the protesters continued to chant, "Varkolak, go home." McCoy felt his fists clench involuntarily, and the doctor part of his brain unconsciously diagnosed his agitated condition as his hypothalamus releasing oxytocin and vasopressin, and his pituitary gland producing large amounts of adrenocorticotropic hormones. In layman's terms, he was plain mad as hell.

McCoy pointed a finger in Daagen's face. "If we'd had your attitude a hundred years ago, your race wouldn't even *be* in the Federation."

"A specious argument, Dr. McCoy. Tellar Prime was a founding member of the Federation. We could hardly have been denied access if there was no Federation to join."

McCoy fumed. "Damn stubborn Tellarites and your nitpicky arguments! You know what I mean."

"There is a clear and accepted application process for joining the Federation, Dr. McCoy, and any race who sees the wisdom in joining the Federation will be welcome."

"And any who don't?"

The Tellarite put his IF YOU'RE NOT WITH US, YOU'RE AGAINST US sign in McCoy's face. McCoy moved to rip it from Daagen's hands, but Nadja was there to stop him.

"Don't. Come on. You're not going to win an argument with a Tellarite," she told him.

"Listen to your lady friend, Dr.," Daagen told him. He nodded at Mrs. Penelope. "Are you going to eat all of that dog?"

"I'll give you something to eat," Bones said. He wagged his fist at the Tellarite.

Nadja pulled McCoy away. "Down, boy. Are you always so easily excitable?"

"Only when I run into damn fool idiots!" he said,

making sure the last part was loud enough to carry back to the protesters.

McCoy calmed down some on the short walk back to Nadja's dorm, but he was still worked up over Daagen. Such backward thinking, and from a Starfleet cadet, no less!

Nadja stopped outside the lobby to her dormitory and let Mrs. Penelope down to sniff the marigolds planted beside the sidewalk. Nadja put her hands behind her back and bounced ever so slightly on the balls of her feet.

"So. Here we are," she said.

Here they were. At the door to her dormitory. *Good god, it's the end of the date*, McCoy realized. The end of a date was as important as the auto-suture at the end of a surgery—and had to be planned just as carefully. There was the small talk to plan, the next date to line up, and, if the operation had been a success, the good-night kiss. Or perhaps even more. How on Earth had they gotten to this point without him seeing it coming?

"Right," he said, realizing he'd been quiet for too long. "Here we are."

"My roommate's pulling an all-nighter in the astro-metric lab tonight, in case you'd like to come upstairs for . . . a nightcap."

McCoy really had meant to prepare for this. It was that damned Daagen, getting him all worked up. He took a deep breath. He and Nadja hadn't gotten around to the last

two decades of *his* life or to the part about his ex-wife. His *recent* ex-wife. Damn it— Why the hell hadn't he prepared for any of this? He looked up at the dorm room windows, as if he could see the future through them.

"Listen, Nadja, I . . . I appreciate the offer. Believe me. I had a terrific time, and I'd like to see you again. Soon. But I think for now, I need to just leave it at 'good night.'"

"Ooh! Now you are playing hard to get." She laughed, but it was a good laugh. "A man who can go against instinct. I'm impressed."

Nadja kissed him good night and scooped up Mrs. Penelope.

"Until next time," she said, and she went inside.

"Until next time," McCoy said.

CH.05.30
Special Relationships

Nyota Uhura paced the small confines of the Academy observation deck. The lights in the room were dim at night, so visitors could see the lights of Sausalito across the water from the Academy grounds. Uhura thought the lighting was appropriate. She was both literally and figuratively in the dark, and while she wasn't eager for the lights to be turned on in the observation deck, she was certainly hoping some light would be shed on a different, and very puzzling, part of her life.

The turbolift at the other end of the room *ding*ed and opened, and Spock stepped out.

"Commander Spock!" she said, practically running across the room to him.

"Please. Just Spock," he reminded her. They had recently agreed to call each other by their first names when not in uniform. Or in Spock's case, the only part of his name Uhura knew. He had assured her that his full name was unpronounceable for most humans, even a linguist of Uhura's ability.

"Spock, what's this all about?" Uhura asked.

"Were you followed on the way here?" Spock asked her. "Did you tell anyone where you were going or with whom you were meeting?"

"What? No. I wasn't followed. At least I don't think so. And no, I didn't tell anyone where I was going. Spock, what's going on? Who were those jokers in the robes, and why were you with them?"

Spock moved to the observation window, standing with his hands clasped behind his back. Uhura could see the reflection of his face in the glass as he stared at Fort Baker and the bay in the distance.

"Those 'jokers,' as you put it, are a very real, and very powerful, organization within the Academy and Starfleet, and the Federation at large. There is evidence that the group is as old as the Federation itself."

"The Graviton Society. Ready to do what the Federation can't or won't do for itself."

"Yes. No doubt you understand the derivation of their name—gravitons are the key component of deflector shields. That is how the society sees itself. They are the individual particles that make up a larger shield, which protects the Federation from outside threats."

"Because Starfleet isn't strong enough already," Uhura said sarcastically.

"They believe not. Or rather, they believe that Starfleet could be made stronger."

"And you believe this?"

"I believe there is always room for improvement in any endeavor, but that is not why I sought an invitation." Spock turned. "I am on a special assignment for Captain Pike. He has tasked me to infiltrate the Graviton Society, and, if it proves dangerous, to expose it."

"Aha!" said Uhura, relieved at last. "That explains it. You're undercover!"

"Yes. But I must confess that having spent some time now as a member of the society, I have yet to discover anything so damning, they must be stopped."

"A secret organization that works outside the rules of Starfleet, Spock? How can that not be dangerous? It runs counter to everything Starfleet stands for."

Spock frowned. "I agree there is the potential for danger if the society goes too far. But it is true the Federation often makes decisions based on emotional stimuli—intangibles, like loyalty, trust, and honor—when an application of logic would be more beneficial. How many times has the Federation made a treaty or pact with a nonaligned race, only to have the nonaligned world go back on the agreement the moment it suits their purposes? And even if we do not invite conflict with our more belligerent neighbors, the reality is that such conflicts still arise and sometimes prove to be beyond the effects of diplomacy. Is it not prudent to defer such eventualities in any way possible, even if those methods are somewhat . . . disingenuous?"

"Methods, like, say, assassination?"

Spock blinked. "There is no evidence that the Graviton Society has ever engaged in such extreme measures. Do you have reason to suspect—"

"No, Spock. It's just an example. But assassination, sabotage, political destabilization—they're just a small slide down that slippery slope. We're supposed to be the bright, shining example for the rest of the galaxy. We're *Starfleet*."

"But I will remind you," said Spock, "that our enemies have no such standards."

"Trust me on this one, Spock. This little game the Graviton Society is playing? People are going to get hurt. Maybe not now, but soon. Innocent people, Spock. In Africa they have a saying: When elephants fight, it is the grass that suffers."

Spock looked like he was mulling over the expression, no doubt trying to remember what an Earth elephant looked like. "An apt metaphor," he said at last. "But there is also an appropriate Vulcan adage: The needs of the many outweigh the needs of the one, or the few."

"So if one or two people lose their liberty—or worse, their lives—it's a fair trade for the safety of billions?"

"It is only logical."

Uhura's heart sank. She and Spock had been growing so close lately. She would never have thought she'd be attracted to a Vulcan. They were usually so haughty, so disdainful of other races. But Spock had been different. Spock had been . . . well, more human than the rest, despite his best efforts. Or perhaps he had secretly embraced the parts of him that were human, and Uhura had been able to see them because she was looking where others didn't— and more carefully. She stared at Spock now with an ache down deep in her chest, in that place that has no name and appears on no medical chart, that place that cannot be sated except by an equal and opposite ache in another. She hurt because she knew then that she was in love with Spock—and understood, at the same moment, that she could never love anyone who could sacrifice innocent lives for the greater good.

Uhura turned away. "You sound like you've already made up your mind, then."

She felt Spock's hand on her shoulder, and that place in her chest fluttered. "I know," he said. "Which is why I suggested they invite you to join the society. I need you, Nyota."

She turned. They were close now. Close enough for her to feel the rise and fall of his chest, to reach out and lay her palm there and feel the beating of his half-human, half-Vulcan heart. But there was still too wide a gulf of duty and propriety and fear between them for her to do that. They stood as close as two people could without touching and held each other with their eyes instead.

"You need me?" Uhura asked.

"I believe the society may be shielding me from the truth of their more illicit activities, either because I am a Vulcan or because they know me to be loyal to Starfleet. Captain Pike worried that might be the case and authorized me to select any . . . 'agents' I deemed necessary. It is my hope that, should you accept their invitation, you will eventually become more involved in the Graviton Society's inner workings and thus help me better fulfill my mission."

"Oh," Uhura said. So the way Spock needed her was not the way she needed him. The place in her chest ached even more. She needed to get away. To be alone. *Now.*

"All right," she said. "I'll do it." She turned and walked as fast as she could toward the turbolift without looking like she was running away. Mercifully, the turbolift doors opened when she pushed the button. She hurried inside.

"Nyota, for this operation to be as successful as possible, we should do everything we can to keep our . . . special relationship . . . as secret as possible," Spock told her.

Uhura nodded without turning around. As the turbolift

doors closed behind her, she wondered exactly what sort of special relationship Spock thought they had and what sort of special relationship they might have shared had the galaxy been a very different place.

Jim Kirk pulled back into the shadows of the hedgerow as a trio of girls walked by, heading back to Nimitz Hall for the night. He recognized one of them, Cadet Rixtar, from Dr. Gill's Federation history class. Staring at the back of her was the reason he'd gotten an A minus instead of an A last semester. Kirk caught something in their conversation about a yak and a rubber hose, but lost the rest of it as they passed by, laughing. He felt a bit of a voyeur, watching people who didn't know they were being watched. If anyone had discovered him in the bushes right then, it would have taken a lot of explaining to get out of this one.

Kirk turned the gold Academy badge with Ard Jarikar's name on it over and over again in his hand. He had a lot of other things he needed to be doing right now, but after a surreptitious interview with Jarikar's roommate—and a small donation of twenty credits—he had learned that tonight was the night Jarikar had a late Parrises Square practice. None of the rest of Jarikar's teammates lived in Nimitz Hall with him, so Kirk had positioned himself in the one place he could hide where Jarikar would pass him alone.

Unless he walked back to Nimitz with someone else. Or there was someone else on the sidewalk nearby to see them and prevent Kirk from "assassinating" Jarikar. Or unless Jarikar decided to head to the cafeteria for a late-night snack or to the library or to the science lab or—

Someone came walking down the path, and Kirk crouched low in the shadows again. Big thudding footsteps, the clack of plastic on plastic, a hummed Orion space shanty, and the lumbering hulk of Ard Jarikar stepped into the circle of the streetlight a few meters away from where Kirk lay in wait. Jarikar was one of the biggest cadets on campus, easily two meters tall and weighing in at 130 kilograms, nearly all of which was muscle. His Orion skin was as green as a watermelon, clashing with his red Parrises Square uniform. The padding in the outfit made him look even bigger.

But he was alone, and that was all that mattered.

Kirk waited until Jarikar stepped out of the light, just in case anyone was watching, and leaped out in front of the Orion.

"Ha-HA!" Kirk said, feeling a bit like a swashbuckler. He waved his spork like a fencing foil and waggled Jarikar's badge for him to see. "Tag, Jarikar. You're it."

To the big Orion's credit, he didn't jump or start or cry out in surprise. Maybe there wasn't much that scared you if you went through life two meters tall and weighing 130 kilograms, Kirk figured.

"Hand over whosever badge you've got, Jarikar. You're dead."

Jarikar slid the plastic carrying case for his ion mallet off his shoulders and tossed it in the grass. Then, to Kirk's growing dismay, the big Orion smiled.

"I'd like to point out—merely as a technicality, of course, Kirk—that you have yet to actually touch me with the spork."

Kirk looked at the little spork in his hand, then up at the big Orion. The big 130-kilogram Orion wearing Parrises Square pads. Ard Jarikar cracked his knuckles and lowered himself into an Andorian martial-arts fighting position.

"Aw, man. This isn't how things were supposed to go down at all." Kirk moaned. "I was supposed to be spending the night with Cadet Areia."

Ard Jarikar nodded. "Deltans. The only thing better than Orion girls."

Kirk sighed, gave a crazed yell, and charged.

CH.06.30
Public Indecency

Kirk reported early the next morning for his first day of babysitting the Varkolak doctor, Lartal. His encounter with Ard Jarikar the night before had been a painful experience. His left knee ached, his cheeks were puffed and bruised, and he was pretty sure one of his ribs was cracked. But it had all been worth it. In his pocket was Jarikar's next target in the Assassination Game—now *his* next target.

Kirk's good mood was snuffed out when he saw his least favorite chief waiting for him outside the Varkolak compound.

"Kirk, you look like hell," the boorish officer told him. "What happened?"

"I walked into an Orion," Kirk said.

"You should see a doctor."

"I did," Kirk told him. Well, he'd seen Bones, at least. McCoy had insisted on giving him a once-over with his medical tricorder, to make sure there hadn't been any damage to his internal organs, and he'd fixed Kirk's sprained wrist at the same time. Sometimes it really did pay to have a doctor as a roommate.

"You should see a better one, then," Hard-Ass told him. "But not now. You're expected inside the kennel. Here. Me and the boys got you a little something."

The chief pressed a studded dog collar into Kirk's hands, and the two security officers by the door laughed.

The door to the Varkolak compound slid open, and there stood a ferocious-looking wolf-man with a white ring of fur around his neck. Lartal.

The security officers stopped laughing, and Kirk hastily stuffed the collar into his pocket.

"Kirk," Lartal said, growling his *R*s. "You are on time. Good." Lartal sniffed disdainfully at the chief, baring his teeth. "Leave us!"

The chief swallowed a comeback. "Good luck, Kirk," the chief told him. He glanced at where Kirk had hidden away the collar. "Be sure to use that if they go chasing after hovercars."

The chief left, and Kirk stepped inside. Lartal and two Varkolak—the same two who had been with Lartal in the conference room? It was hard to tell—were in a small common room shared by four bedrooms. The room smelled like wet dog, and there was hair all over the furniture.

Lartal gestured to the table. "Would you like some breakfast?"

Kirk saw the plates of raw meat, and his stomach turned. "No, thanks. I just ate," he lied.

The other two Varkolak laughed, like hyenas, but they quieted when Lartal shot them a look.

"Your chief. His comment about hovercars and the leather strap he gave you. It is a reference of some kind to the domesticated canines of your world?"

Quick decision, thought Kirk. *Lie or tell the truth?*

"Yes," Kirk said. He took the collar out of his pocket and tossed it onto the table. "It's a dog collar. On Earth, dogs are notorious for chasing anything that moves. Especially cars."

The other two Varkolak sneered and growled, but Lartal silenced them. He nodded. "Good. Let there be no lies between us, Kirk. You dislike us, and we dislike you. I asked for you because you do not hide behind words, like your chief. And unlike all the other humans, you do not reek of fear."

"What can I say? They were all out when I went into the perfume store."

Dr. Lartal picked up something that looked like a tricorder from a table at the back of the room, hooking it onto his belt. Kirk wondered if it was one of the incredibly accurate sensing devices the Varkolak were famous for. The only thing the Federation knew about how they worked was that they used kemocite for a power source. The rest was a mystery—one Federation scientists salivated over.

"I am ready to leave," Lartal said.

Kirk wasn't looking forward to this—not because he would be escorting a Varkolak around all day, but because it was going to be *boring*. The medical conference didn't start until tomorrow, thankfully, but Starfleet had arranged for tours of the Academy's medical research facilities today for all the attendees. Kirk was in for a day of medical discussions and biobed demonstrations. Why couldn't Bones have been the one Lartal wanted?

"All right," Kirk said. "The first tour of the morning is the obstetrics facility. After that, we've got the psychiatric facility, then the—"

"No," Lartal said. "I would like a tour of the campus."

"You . . . don't want to go on the medical tours?"

Lartal frowned. At least, Kirk took his expression to be a frown. "No. Come."

The two other Varkolak stood to go with them, but Lartal told them to remain behind. They whimpered objections, but he barked something in Varkolak, and they sat back down at the table.

All right, then, Kirk thought as Lartal marched past him out of the room. *Maybe I'm going to need that leash after all.*

Hikaru Sulu's helm console lit up like Shibuya at night. Red-alert klaxons wailed and the bridge shook as the inertial dampeners tried to compensate for the phaser blasts raining down on the *Yorktown*.

"Heading one-one-three, mark eight!" Viktor Tikhonov shouted from the captain's chair. "Evasive maneuvers! Pattern gamma four!"

"Heading one-one-three, mark eight, evasive maneuvers, pattern gamma four, aye!" Sulu confirmed, putting the coordinates into the helm.

"Four more Varkolak ships approaching from starboard, bearing zero-nine-three, mark ten!" Pavel Chekov announced from his position at ops, just to the right of Sulu. Chekov pronounced his *V*s like *W*s—"Warkolak" instead of "Varkolak"—something Sulu had long since gotten used to after dozens of missions at the Russian's side.

"They're surrounding us!" Tikhonov cried.

Of course they're surrounding us, you idiot, Sulu thought. *That's what the Varkolak do.* The Constitution-class *Yorktown* was bigger and stronger than any single Varkolak ship, but the way the Varkolak brought down bigger prey was to circle it and harry it until it went down under the fire of a dozen smaller ships.

"Shields at seventy percent," Chekov said.

"Return fire! Target the lead ship!" Tikhonov ordered.

"But which one is the lead ship?" Chekov asked.

That's it, isn't it? Sulu thought as he twisted the *Yorktown* out of the path of a photon torpedo. The Varkolak most certainly had an alpha. Everything they'd been taught about them said they were a pack-dominated society. One of those ships was the alpha, and the others were just betas, following the leader. That's what made the Varkolak such difficult enemies—they were always perfectly in sync with one another and never broke ranks. But what if the betas were betas for a reason?

Sulu broke off his heading and swung the *Yorktown* around at the nearest Varkolak ship. The *Yorktown* rocked as the pursuing Varkolak ships bore down on them, firing phasers in close quarters.

"No, no!" Tikhonov yelled. "Evasive maneuvers! Pattern . . . pattern . . ."

Sulu didn't bother to wait for Tikhonov to make up his mind. He plowed into the cluster of Varkolak ships, breaking their line. Two of them peeled away. Emboldened, Sulu turned the prow of the *Yorktown* into the rest of the pack, scattering more ships. Soon the Varkolak would regroup and come at the *Yorktown* again, but hopefully, in the meantime—

"Got him!" Chekov said. Only one dog hadn't been sent scurrying away by the charge of the great moose that was the *Yorktown*. A single ship that was identical to all the others in every respect save one—its captain was the alpha leader. He alone kept his ship in the fight against overwhelming odds, because that's what made him an alpha leader.

It was so obvious even Tikhonov could see it. "There! Target that ship!" he ordered, but he needn't have bothered. Chekov had already sent two photon torpedoes screaming toward the Varkolak cruiser. They hit the little Varkolak ship dead-on, knocking out its shields and destroying one of its warp nacelles. It listed in space, critically wounded and venting plasma.

"The other Varkolak ships are breaking off their attack and going to warp," Chekov announced. "We have won!"

Sulu's helm console went blank, the red-alert klaxons died, and the bridge crew breathed a collective sigh of relief as the lights came up and the simulation came to an end. One or two even clapped.

The door to the observation room opened, and their Academy instructors came into the room, led by Commander Spock.

"Congratulations," Spock said. "The Varkolak are a difficult and implacable enemy. Your approach to the battle was both novel and effective."

Chekov shot Sulu a congratulatory smile.

"Thank you," Tikhonov told Commander Spock. "I

knew if we could just isolate the lead ship from the others, we could rout them."

Chekov frowned. "But you would never have known which ship was the leader if Sulu hadn't—" he began, but Sulu shook his head to silence him.

"Your bridge crew is to be commended," Spock said. "Dismissed."

Chekov hung back with Sulu and watched Tikhonov leave, regaling one of the female cadets from their simulation crew with tales of his amazing prowess at command.

"You should not let that Cossack take credit for your work," Chekov told Sulu. "You are the reason we won today, not him."

Sulu nodded his thanks. "I'll let my grades and my record do the talking for me."

Chekov shook his head, but relented. Chekov was the closest thing Sulu had to a friend at the Academy, but Sulu had resisted the young Russian's attempts to get him out of his study carrel in the astrometric building. After a while, Chekov had gotten the hint and stopped asking.

Together they went into the next room, where the other cadets were collecting their things. Sulu watched as they paired off to leave, eying each other suspiciously, and then he remembered the game some of them were playing. The Assassination Game, they called it. He'd seen the signs in the student center and had been interested, but he'd never really seriously considered joining. He wasn't at the Academy to make friends or to play games. He was here to work hard, study hard, and graduate with a top posting. There wasn't time for anything else.

"Cadet Sulu, if I might have a word with you?" Commander Spock said.

"Yes, sir. Of course."

Sulu and Chekov nodded their good-byes, and Spock waited until he and Sulu were alone.

"Your superior piloting skills today did not go unnoticed," Commander Spock remarked.

Sulu straightened. "Thank you, sir."

"I understand you will also be piloting the shuttle that brings the president of the United Federation of Planets to tomorrow's opening ceremonies for the Interspecies Medical Summit. A well-deserved honor. With your skills at helm and your excellent grades in astrophysics, you should have your pick of positions upon graduation."

Sulu almost didn't know what to say. He'd never received this much praise from an instructor—particularly from a Vulcan. "Thank you, sir."

Commander Spock glanced around, as if to make sure no one else was with them.

"Cadet, you are about to receive an invitation. An exceedingly *odd* invitation," Spock told him.

"Sir? What kind of invitation?"

"That, I cannot say. It may be an offer you are interested in. If it is not, I would appreciate you speaking to me before you say no."

"I— All right," Sulu said, absolutely mystified.

"Thank you, Cadet," said Commander Spock, and he left Sulu alone to gather his things.

What in the world had that all been about? Sulu cycled up his PADD as he walked across campus to his carrel in the astrometric building, but a strange message in his inbox stopped him in his tracks:

CADET HIKARU SULU, PLEASE COME ALONE TO ROOM 219, VANDERBILT HALL, TONIGHT AT 2300 HOURS. The request had no sender, and was signed only with what Sulu recognized as a two-dimensional rendering of a graviton particle.

An exceedingly odd invitation indeed.

Dr. Lartal's tour of the Academy grounds had quickly turned into an off-campus excursion into the nearby Golden Gate Park. Kirk wasn't sure what was guiding the Varkolak's wanderings, but he suspected it had something to do with the Varkolak's nose. He seemed far more interested in sniffing the air than he did in seeing any of the sights Kirk pointed out.

"And there's the . . . Golden Gate Bridge," Kirk said, petering out when it was clear Lartal had absolutely no interest in one of Earth's most well-known landmarks. Kirk shrugged and shared a bewildered look with the two Starfleet Security officers who accompanied them. All around them, the throngs of tourists out on what was a gorgeously sunny summer day in San Francisco gave them a wide berth. More than one set of parents hustled their young children away from the Varkolak.

Lartal sniffed at a park bench, utterly unfazed by either the view or the nervous people around him. "Your face," he said to Kirk without looking up. "It is injured. And you walk today with a limp you did not have yesterday."

Thanks for noticing, Kirk thought. "Yeah. My ribs aren't in such great shape either," Kirk told him. "The chief said I need to see a doctor. Maybe you want to take a look."

"Not particularly, no," Lartal said. He moved from the bench to one of the telescopes along the rail at the edge of the Marin Headlands, the sea of tourists parting for him like subspace around a warp field.

Now that was odd, Kirk thought. According to Bones, every doctor from here to Romulus wanted to get a proper body scan of a Varkolak, and Kirk had to assume the reverse was true of every Varkolak doctor—as well as just about every doctor from every member race of the Federation. He'd just offered Dr. Lartal a chance to give him a full body scan, and the Varkolak had turned it down.

If Lartal really *was* a doctor. Kirk was beginning to doubt that more and more.

Lartal pulled the sensor device off his belt and held it up like he was scanning the area.

"Whoa, whoa, whoa!" Kirk said, hurrying over. Letting a member of a race with whom the Federation currently shared an uneasy détente sweep the area near Starfleet Command with a scanner seemed like a very, *very* bad idea. "I don't, uh, I don't think you should be . . ." Kirk said, suddenly realizing how little authority he had over the Varkolak. Before he could enlist the help of the security officers, Lartal was pointing across the bay to San Francisco.

"I wish to go there," Lartal said.

Kirk was taken aback. He wanted to go into the city? Why? Did Lartal's decision have something to do with the scan he'd just done? Downtown San Francisco was something like seven or eight kilometers away. Kirk knew the Varkolak sensor technology was legendary, but no handheld scanner could have picked up anything at that range.

Could it?

"Well, sure," Kirk said. "I suppose." He looked to the two Starfleet Security officers, to see if there was an official objection, but they were just as stumped as Kirk was. "Why?"

Lartal's tongue lolled out over his sharp teeth, and Kirk wondered if the Varkolak had to pant like a dog to regulate his body temperature under all that fur.

"To . . . sightsee," Lartal said with a wolfish grin.

Right, Kirk thought. *Because you've been so interested in the sights so far.*

"All right. Well, your wish is my command. Whenever you're ready, we can catch a ferry over to the city."

Lartal put a foot up on one of the benches that overlooked the bay and the bridge. Kirk thought the Varkolak was taking one last look at the impressive vista before leaving, but then he heard a hissing sound, and realized Lartal had sprayed something on the bench.

"Whoa! Hey, no! What are you— No graffiti!" Kirk said.

"I have not permanently marked it," Lartal said. "Merely added my own personal scent to"—the Varkolak sniffed—"the human *fetor* that already exists in this place. It will not linger more than a few days. Now, take me to the city."

Kirk shook his head. This was going to be one *long* afternoon.

●　·　·　✦　∶·　✦　·　✦　··　·

Bones was at his desk in the room they shared when Kirk got back at the end of the day. Kirk hadn't kept track, but Lartal had to have walked at least twenty kilometers all over San Francisco, and those weren't flat kilometers either. Kirk collapsed facedown onto his bed.

"Bones, you will not believe the kind of day I've had. First, Lartal skips out on the medical tours. Then we check out the Marin Headlands, where he sprays Varkolak perfume on a bench. Then we go into San Francisco, where he howled on every other street corner and spritzed every other trash can and light pole with his scent. I didn't know if we were going to get a ticket for vandalism or disturbing the peace, or both. In the end, I think the cops were so scared of him, they just said, 'It's Starfleet's deal' and left it to us."

"That's interesting," Bones said in a tone that made it sound like it was anything but.

Kirk shifted to look at him. Bones was staring off into space.

"And then Lartal ate a baby," Kirk said, just to see if Bones was listening. "Just snatched it right up out of a baby carriage and wolfed it down."

"Uh-huh," Bones said. "Listen, Jim, I think I'm ready to get back on the horse. With Nadja."

"Ah. I see." Kirk sat up on his bed. "Well, first, I recommend you not use that expression when you tell her the same thing."

"I'm serious, Jim. It's taken me a long time to get over Jocelyn, but I think it's time."

"I couldn't agree more, Bones. Got a first date all planned out?"

"We already kind of had one. We took her dog for a walk out along the Marin Headlands."

Kirk chuckled—he'd done much the same thing today. "Listen, Bones, taking a dog for a walk is not romantic in the least. You need something with candles and wine and stars next time."

"Yeah," Bones said, like he had an idea. "Wait a minute. *Did you just tell me that Varkolak doctor ate a baby?*"

"I was joking. But not about the other stuff." Kirk leaned back wearily on his bed. "I'm not the right guy for this job, Bones. I don't want to be this guy's handler."

"No—no. This is a golden opportunity for interspecies understanding, Jim. This is a big deal. You know how many Federation diplomats would love to have the chance you've got right now, to reach out to the Varkolak and find common ground?"

"Common ground? Bones, I'm lucky the man didn't lift his leg at something."

"Jim, you're the right man for the job because the Varkolak *picked* you. That's half the battle right there, getting them to trust one of us. God knows there aren't enough of us who trust them. And if you don't do it for the sake of interstellar relations, do it for your service record, Jim. Your record's spotty enough as it is. You need a win here, a gold star to balance out all those black *X*s."

"Thanks," Kirk said, but he knew Bones was right.

"Look, the next time this Lartal wants to go out somewhere, share with him something *you* like to do. At least then you'll have a good time. Maybe even stay out of trouble. If he even leaves campus again. The medical conference starts tomorrow, and he'll be tied up with seminars all day and official receptions all night."

"All right. Yeah. Thanks, Bones," Kirk said, although he wondered again if Lartal really was the doctor he claimed to be. And if he wasn't, what was he doing here?

CH.07.30
Opening Ceremonies

Uhura turned on the sonic shower and sighed in relief as the pulse vibrations massaged her, removing the sweat and grime from her morning workout in the Academy Sports Complex. She'd pushed herself extra hard this morning, and she knew she would pay for it later. Probably while she was standing on the dais with the linguistics team, helping to translate the Federation president's remarks.

Stupid.

She'd told herself it was just to step up her regimen, but here in the privacy of her sonic shower stall, alone with nothing but her thoughts, she knew the truth of it. She'd worked herself to the point of exhaustion, trying to exorcise the demons that had kept her up all night. How could he be so blind? Couldn't he see how she looked at him? How she acted around him? And how could she have been so stupid, falling in love with someone who had spent most of his life suppressing his emotions? Someone who didn't know how to return her love? It was easy to picture Spock in place of the punching bag when doing her Suus Mahna practice, but even that hadn't been satisfying. Deep down she knew why: Spock hadn't misled her. She'd misled herself. She'd read more into the commander's offer of friendship than he'd meant. He was a Vulcan, damn it. All right, maybe half-Vulcan, but all Vulcan when it came to the choice of cold hard logic over emotion. She slapped a hand on the softly glowing wall of the sonic shower. How could she have been so stupid?

"Cadet Uhura," someone said, and Uhura jumped.

"Who's there?" Uhura asked.

The blurry shadow of another person appeared on the other side of the frosted wall. It was someone in the next stall, leaning close to the wall that separated them so Uhura could see her silhouette.

"We have received your acceptance to our invitation. Welcome, Cadet Uhura, to the Graviton Society." It was hard to hear whoever it was over the hum of the sonic shower, but Uhura gathered that was kind of the point.

"You could have waited until I was a little more decent."

"The Graviton Society has a mission for you," the shadow in the next stall said. "We wish for you to steal one of the Varkolak's sensing devices."

"*What?* Steal one of their scanners? You've got to be kidding!"

"You have unique access to the Varkolak through your linguistics work. It should be possible."

"But it's wrong! They're our guests. I mean, I know they're our enemies, too, but—"

"You joined the Graviton Society to protect the Federation, Cadet Uhura. Are you backing out on that decision?"

"I— No," she grumbled. This was definitely not what she'd had in mind when she'd agreed to go undercover in the Graviton Society, but now she was committed. "I'll see what I can do."

"The Graviton Society expects success," the woman told her. "Shields up."

Uhura assumed that was some sort of society sign off. The shadow disappeared from the wall, and the door to the next shower stall banged shut.

"Shields up," Uhura said to the empty stall, still feeling exposed. She was going to have to talk to Spock about this, which meant she was going to have to see him again sooner than she wanted to. Uhura sighed and cranked up the sonic pitch as high as it would go.

The red-orange tops of the Golden Gate Bridge stuck up out of a sea of fog that morning as McCoy found himself standing at the tip of the Marin Headlands for the second time in two days. He was there with other top medical cadets at the invitation of Starfleet Medical, as part of the official opening ceremonies for the Interspecies Medical Summit. The dais where the Federation president was due to speak was arranged so the crowd would have the best possible view of the bridge and the bay beyond, but, of course, today the weather hadn't cooperated. With a scowl, McCoy wondered if they might even get rained on.

We can travel faster than the speed of light, and break a person down to bits and transport him through space, but we still can't control the weather, McCoy groused to himself, but truth be told, he was a little glad of that. There ought to be some things that always remained outside their control, just to remind them they weren't the masters of the universe. Being omnipotent would just make most people more insufferable.

The part of the overlook usually open to the public had been roped off for the ceremony, and classes had been suspended for the morning, so the Academy could show up en masse for the president's speech. At a guess, McCoy would say most of them were here, though some he knew would take the opportunity to get caught up on their homework. Or their sleep. There were dignitaries here too—doctors and politicians from nearly every Federation member world, and plenty more besides. The Varkolak were there as well, and McCoy wondered how many of the cadets had come out just for the chance to see their mysterious visitors. Jim Kirk stepped up onto the dais with the white-collared Varkolak, Dr. Lartal, and McCoy nodded hello from across the stage. If Kirk played his cards right with this one, he could win himself some major points with the Academy brass—and better, the Starfleet brass.

"Oh good. I see we're letting the *krogs* into the *vorsch* pit now," said a sarcastic voice from behind McCoy. He turned. It was Daagen, the medical cadet McCoy had seen here the night before, waving a VARKOLAK, GO HOME sign. McCoy took his comment to be a Tellarite expression, along the lines of letting a fox into the henhouse, but he didn't challenge him. Not here. Not now. The Varkolak just being here was argument enough against Daagen's xeno-phobic attitude.

McCoy saw another familiar face: Cadet Uhura, doing some kind of a wiggling dance in front of one of the Varkolak doctors. He realized it was a form of communication only when the doctor she'd been dancing for started barking and dancing in response. Now *there* was somebody who would actually change the face of the galaxy one day, he thought. Not a doctor or an engineer or a starship captain, but a lin-guist. Someone who could bridge the biggest gap facing interplanetary peace: simply understanding what the devil everyone else was talking about.

Someone pointed, and McCoy saw a shuttle flying over the fog bank from San Francisco. The Federation president was on her way. On the dais, the various groups awaiting her arrival hurried to their places, pulling on tunics and straightening their hair or fur or antennae. Federation News Service reporters scrambled into position, and McCoy caught sight of Nadja Luther among a group of engineering cadets ready to help receive the shuttle and prep it for its return trip. *The gang's all here*, he thought, and he couldn't help staring at her until the descending shuttle cut her off from view.

The craft touched down far more smoothly than any shuttle McCoy had ever ridden in, but then he wasn't Pellan Fel, president of the United Federation of Planets. She emerged wearing a dark-blue pantsuit in the military fashion favored by Andorians and nodded her thanks to her Japanese pilot, a cadet McCoy hadn't met. Starfleet's Chief Medical Officer, Admiral Cindy Wójcik, welcomed the president and escorted her to the podium.

"Hail and well met, fellow citizens of the Federation and honored guests from around the galaxy. I come here today as the president of the United Federation of Planets to officially open an historic conference, one that will see the unprecedented attendance of more than two dozen governments, spanning thirty-four sectors and two quadrants, all of whom have come together today in a spirit of understanding and cooperation, to advance that most noble of pursuits, the—"

Pellan Fel never finished. An explosion ripped through the shuttle behind her, and McCoy's world went black.

CH.08.30
Course Changes

Uhura sat in the conference room in the Varkolak compound, picking at the dermal patch on her arm, where shrapnel from the explosion had caught her. She'd been lucky. They all had, apparently, as whatever had caused the explosion had blown out the side of the shuttle away from the dais, and no one had died. If it had been on the other side, though . . .

And not *whatever* had caused the explosion. *Whoever.* Shuttles didn't just explode, especially not shuttles that carried the president of the United Federation of Planets and had security and engineering teams going over them before and after every flight.

"Are you all right, dear?" Dr. Cameron asked. He was the oldest member of the linguistics team, easily eighty years old, and like a father to most of the team. A grandfather. "There is absolutely nothing wrong with sitting this one out after what you've just been through."

"No. No, I'm fine," Uhura told him. Which was true, physically speaking. Mentally, Uhura was not fine. She felt her hand start to shake and hid it under the table. She had never been that close to a terrorist attack before. Never had something just a few meters away from her explode with such force, it threw her to the ground and showered her with debris.

She had never been so close to dying.

She'd died in simulations, of course. Been on her share of bridge crews who'd fought computer versions of Romulans and Varkolak and Klingons, and lost. The simulations were tense. When everything went to hell and your console was busted and the red-alert klaxons wouldn't stop and smoke filled the room, your adrenaline got pumping. And when your ship exploded and the lights came up and you knew you were dead—or would have been in real life—it felt like getting thrown from a playground merry-go-round. But all along you knew it was fiction. Even though you went through the motions, with all the energy and excitement of a real situation, your head still knew it wasn't real.

This was real. The suddenness, the heat, the force of it. The *violation* of it. This was her place. The Academy campus, Fort Baker, Marin county, San Francisco—this was inviolable turf, like home. Things like this weren't supposed to happen here. The explosion had changed everything.

Uhura slid her shaking hand up her arm to her dermal patch again.

The explosion had changed *her*.

A detail of Starfleet Security officers led the big alpha Varkolak, Dr. Lartal, into the room, followed by two of Lartal's Varkolak guards. Uhura felt herself stiffen. She was already sure he had been behind the explosion. Or if not him, one of the other "doctors" or guards visiting under a banner of truce for the conference.

The security officers put Lartal in a seat on the other side of the table, and soon a Starfleet Security officer with commander stripes on his sleeves came in with a PADD and sat down across from him.

"Why am I being detained?" Lartal growled.

"Do I really need to answer that?" asked the commander.

"You blame me for the bombing." Lartal sat back in his chair. "Of course."

"Dr. Lartal, I understand you skipped the tours of the medical facilities yesterday and instead insisted on visiting other locations, including the area where today's incident took place. Why?"

"Sightseeing."

"And yet the security detail with you said you barely paid attention to any of the sights."

Lartal said nothing.

"You weren't scouting locations for a bomb?"

"No."

The commander held the Varkolak's gaze for a moment, then pushed a button on a video console on the table and spun it toward Lartal. "This is footage from one of the FNS cameras filming the speech today." The commander froze the picture. "See here, how you're diving away from the shuttle an instant before anyone else?"

"I do."

"Can you explain how you knew that shuttle was going to explode before anyone else did?"

"My *gutsaina* told me," he said, using a Varkolak word.

"Your what?" The commander looked to the linguist team.

Dr. Cameron was shaking his head at the linguistic console again. "We don't have a direct translation for it."

Uhura heard the Varkolak root word for "scent" in the word and saw the subtle way Lartal's nose twitched as he said it.

"Smeller. Thing that smells? Sniffer," Uhura said. "His scanning device."

The Varkolak turned his wolfish eyes on her again. "Yes." He plucked the scanning device off his belt and put it on the table in front of him—but not close enough for the commander to reach out for it.

"No one near you reported hearing a sound from your . . . 'sniffer.'"

"The sound is inaudible to human ears." His eyes were still on Uhura. "Not even, I think, this one's exceptional ears."

Uhura shuddered under the Varkolak's stare, but didn't look away. His tongue wagged in a wolfish smile, and he looked back at the commander. "My *gutsaina* alerted me to an imminent plasma explosion. I took action."

"I didn't say it was a plasma explosion," the commander remarked.

"No. You probably don't even know yet, do you?" Lartal said. "I know it was a plasma explosion because my *gutsaina* told me."

"And just why was your 'sniffer' on?"

"It is always on."

Uhura didn't believe a bit of it. The Varkolak's "sniffer" just happened to be on and just happened to go off at a frequency humans couldn't hear, and Lartal just happened to jump out of the way before anyone else. She could see the commander wasn't buying it either.

"So. You heard the alert and you jumped out of the way, because you knew there was going to be a plasma explosion."

"Yes."

"Have a lot of experience with explosives, do you, Dr.?"

Lartal bared his teeth at the commander, but said nothing. The commander pointed to the screen again. "You'll notice none of your colleagues knew to jump clear."

"No. They were fortunate. You should have better security."

The Varkolak behind Lartal chuckled, and the commander shifted in his chair. "Well. You can be sure we're going to be watching a lot more carefully from now on, Dr. Lartal. And I'm going to have to ask you to turn over your scanning device."

Lartal picked up his sniffer from the table and clipped it back onto his belt. "No."

The commander stared across the table at Lartal for a long moment.

"I'll ask you again, Dr. Give us your scanning device."

"And again, I say no. Perhaps you are not aware, but Varkolak Prime is not a member of the United Federation of Planets."

"I've heard that, yes," the commander replied, deadpan.

"Then of course you will understand that I am not bound to oblige."

"Nor are we bound to continue to extend our hospitality," the commander said.

"But you have no evidence any Varkolak was responsible for this heinous deed. You would expel us on suspicion alone? Where is the spirit of understanding and cooperation your president spoke of?"

"You could cooperate by giving us your scanning

device," the commander persisted.

Lartal stood. "And you could attempt to take it from me." His voice was suddenly much lower, and Uhura saw in his words a more aggressive posture and delivery. She looked nervously to the commander and wondered if she should caution him.

"But I warn you," Lartal went on. "To do so would be to provoke a response from the Varkolak Assembly. And it will not come in the form of a carefully worded letter."

Whether he heard it in Lartal's words or just decided now was not the time for an international incident, the commander did nothing to further provoke the Varkolak. He turned off the video console and cycled down his PADD. "You and your contingent are hereby restricted to the Academy grounds. Everything else is off-limits," he told the Varkolak.

Lartal growled, which only meant to Uhura that he was more guilty of something. Why would he need access to anything except the campus if he was really here for the medical conference? That he wanted more meant he was here for some other reason, none of which could be good. Uhura stared at the sniffer on Lartal's belt. Spock was right. The rest of the universe didn't play by the same rules. Had the situation been reversed, the Varkolak would have simply taken the scanner from the commander. But Starfleet was going to let a valuable piece of evidence walk right out of the room. And for what? Principles? Moral high ground? How would ethics help them the next time the Varkolak attacked?

The commander left the room, and Dr. Cameron and the other senior linguists packed up their equipment. "Go on back to your room," Dr. Cameron told her. "Your help was invaluable, but go now. Rest. You are more tired than you know."

Uhura held her shaking hand again and nodded. "I will. Thank you, Dr." Lartal and his lackeys left the room, escorted by a complement of Starfleet Security, and Uhura followed along a few steps behind.

"OrrRain nola haRapatzan gu beRe duzan?" one of Lartal's Varkolak guards asked him.

Lartal leaped on the other Varkolak, biting his neck and riding him to the floor. *"Itxi guza engaina!"* Lartal growled, his teeth still clamped around the other Varkolak's throat.

The Starfleet Security officers immediately scrambled to the periphery, phasers pointed at the two Varkolak, but it was over almost as soon as it had begun. Lartal got up and the other Varkolak remained crouched, whimpering, his tail between his legs.

Lartal turned quickly, and Uhura couldn't wipe the shock off her face in time. Lartal's eyes narrowed and he bared his teeth. Lartal knew she alone had understood their words, and Uhura knew she alone was in terrible danger because of it.

Hikaru Sulu woke in the hospital. He lay on a bio bed, his vital signs charted by the mysterious beeps and chirps from the console behind his head. A white plastic screen separated his bed from the rest of the room, but through it he could hear the soft shufflings of doctors and nurses as they tended to other patients.

The explosion. That's why he was here. There had been an explosion at the opening ceremonies. The shuttle—

It came back to him now. Piloting the president of the Federation across the San Francisco Bay; politely answering her questions about his studies before she went back to talking to her advisors; bringing them in for a landing at the overlook. A pretty perfect touch down, if he did say so himself. The president had thanked him when she'd disembarked and then he'd seen to the shutdown sequence and done the requisite pilot's examination of the outside of his vessel after landing. He'd been at the front of the shuttle when it went up, throwing him clear, but showering him with shards of transparent aluminum and duranium.

Sulu tried to sit up, but his whole body was sore, and his chest and arms and face were tight, like he had a sunburn. The beeping behind him became more insistent, and a Tellarite doctor emerged from between the sheets of plastic. He wore an Academy medical uniform, which meant he was a proper doctor, but in rank, still a cadet, like Sulu.

"Mr. Sulu. You're awake. Good. I'm Dr. Daagen. I'm your attending physician. You took a real shot from the explosion."

"What happened? Do they know?"

"No official word yet. But the words on everyone's lips are 'Varkolak terrorist attack.'"

"How bad is it?" Sulu asked.

"No fatalities. Most are like you. You received multiple lacerations to your face, arms, and chest; bruising along your upper sternum; and a broken clavicle. We've patched, treated, and regenerated your respective injuries. You'll make a full recovery. Your face, of course, will look like mine for the rest of your life," said the wrinkled, pug-nosed Tellarite.

Sulu's eyes went wide.

"That's a joke, Cadet."

Sulu closed his eyes, and sighed. "Nice."

"I assure you, on Tellar Prime this face is considered quite handsome."

"Just keep telling yourself that," Sulu joked.

The Tellarite snorted in amusement.

"In all seriousness, you're going to be fine. I'm afraid it's going to put a crimp in your piloting reaction times for a little while. And your fencing."

Sulu moaned. His fencing was the one thing he did that wasn't a part of his grand plan to work hard, study hard, and graduate with a top posting. He competed for the Academy fencing team so he could have sparring partners, but he was really fencing just for himself. To disappear behind that mask and parry, lunge, redouble, riposte. To anticipate, to defend, to advance, to attack. Fencing was the one thing Sulu had in which he could lose himself entirely and put away, if only briefly, his single-minded determination to succeed in Starfleet. It was his own private retreat from the world, and even losing that escape for a short time was enough to shake him.

"Wait," Sulu said. "How did you know I was a fencer?"

"We make it our business to know everything we can about our recruits before we invite them to join," the doctor said quietly. He pulled up his sleeve and showed Sulu a tattoo of a graviton particle. The Graviton Society. This doctor was a member. "After today's attack on the Federation, on *you*, are you more inclined to accept our offer, Cadet?"

Sulu leaned back onto his pillow and stared at the ceiling. The strange summons on his PADD had been an invitation to join a secret society that claimed to protect the

Federation when it couldn't—or wouldn't—protect itself. Sulu had been surprised by the offer and somewhat flattered. He'd heard rumors about the Graviton Society. That they were the real movers and shakers in Starfleet. A cadet with a plan to end up at the helm of one of Starfleet's flagships would do well to become a member. As long as it didn't distract him from his studies.

Sulu had started to call it The Plan—capital *T*, capital *P*. The Plan was to keep his head down, work hard, and graduate with top honors, which would get him any posting he wanted. That's why he didn't fool around with things like the Assassination Game. In helmsman's terms, Sulu's plan was the course he'd laid years ago, and he'd been traveling at maximum warp toward his destination ever since. He'd made course corrections along the way, to stay on target, certainly. But the Assassination Game, fencing—maybe this Graviton Society—were all detours. Course changes. Temporary layovers. And temporary layovers were never profitable. They diverted you from your mission. Made you late. Sometimes kept you from arriving at all.

But there was also duty to consider. Why Sulu had chosen this course in the first place. He couldn't forget that or The Plan became just a long, difficult journey to an empty planet in space.

"I accept," Sulu finally said. "I'm ready to join."

"Good," said Daagen. "I thought you might. I will be your contact from now on, and I already have a mission for you, Mr. Sulu. There is a mole inside the society, and we're going to dig it out."

CH.09.30
Human Courtship Behavior

It was late in the afternoon by the time Kirk finally saw the sun again. Where had the day gone? Well, there had been the business of escorting Lartal to the opening ceremonies overlooking the Golden Gate Bridge . . . and then the explosion. And the brief period of unconsciousness—that had to account for some of the time, of course. And then the hovering doctors who wouldn't let him leave the hospital because of a few scratches and bruises, and the waiting security team who wouldn't let him leave before asking him a few questions. Five times over. His stomach growled and his feet changed course toward the dining hall without him even thinking about it.

Starfleet Security had wanted to know everything he heard and saw before, during, and after the explosion, and Kirk had told them everything he could remember. What did Lartal do at the overlook when they visited yesterday? Mostly sniff around and mark park benches. Had he done anything suspicious in San Francisco? Just howl on street corners. Had Lartal acted suspicious the morning before the explosion? No more than usual. Did Kirk hear any sound at all from Lartal's "sniffer" before the explosion? No. Did Lartal detonate the bomb?

That was the million-credit question, wasn't it? They wanted Kirk to be able to answer the question definitively, but he couldn't. Yes, there was circumstantial evidence, and yes, they'd shown him the images of Lartal jumping out of the way before the explosion happened, but Kirk had neither seen nor heard anything that made him think Lartal had set off the explosion himself. And, he had to confess, Lartal's leap had caught up Kirk and dragged him out of the way of the blast. Had Lartal tried to save him from the explosion, or had he just bumped him by accident? And what about Kirk's growing suspicion—and Starfleet's too, now—that Lartal wasn't a doctor at all?

Kirk was so lost in his own thoughts, he nearly ran into the cadet who appeared in his way on the sidewalk. Metal flashed as the cadet's hand swiped at him. Kirk's instincts kicked in, and he leaped back out of the way just in time.

Finnegan.

"I looked up corbomite, Kirk." The big cadet advanced on him. Kirk glanced around for someone who could see them and keep Finnegan from being able to tag him with his spork, but they were alone.

"Oh, yeah?" Kirk said, stalling for time as he calculated his next move. "Who taught you how to use a computer?"

Finnegan lunged at him, and Kirk danced out of the way.

"There's no such thing as corbomite," Finnegan said.

"No kidding," Kirk said. "Then I am *definitely* going to have a talk with my exochemistry teacher. I don't think he knows what he's talking about."

"Keep joking, Jimmy boy," Finnegan told him. "I'm just gonna pound you harder."

"All right. You want to do this now?" Kirk said. He crouched in a karate ready position. "Let's do this."

Finnegan grinned and took a step closer.

Kirk turned and ran.

"Come back here, you coward!" Finnegan called, giving chase.

"It's called a tactical retreat!" Kirk yelled back at him. All he had to do was find someone, *anyone*, to latch on to and Finnegan couldn't knock him out of the Assassination Game. Finnegan was big and heavy, but he was all muscle, and he kept up with Kirk well enough for Kirk to keep running. But where the hell *was* everyone? There were thousands of cadets on campus, and hundreds more instructors, not to mention all the doctors here for the conference. They couldn't *all* be at dinner!

"When I catch you, Kirk, I'm gonna stick this spork where the sun don't shine!" Finnegan bellowed.

Kirk ducked into the student center. There were always people there studying, eating, playing dom-jot. He slid to a stop among the dozen or so tables in the lobby. The *empty* lobby.

"The assassination attempt!" Kirk said, finally realizing what was going on. "The whole campus must be on lock-down!"

Finnegan burst in through the front doors, and Kirk dashed out the side exit. There was a bar just off campus, the Warp Core, where cadets went when they wanted to spend a little downtime out of uniform. There had to be someone there—the bartender, Bom, if no one else. Finnegan came at his flank, doubling back on him, and Kirk barely ducked his spork in time. He sprinted with what energy he had left down past Hawking Hall and into the little street where a flickering neon sign announced, THE WARP CORE: HOME OF THE WARP CORE BREACH. Kirk threw himself against the door and came to an ungraceful stop against an empty table.

"Well. I knew Academy life is rough, but I've never seen anybody need a drink that bad," said the Bolian bartender.

"Blue man! I have never been so glad to see you in all my life," Kirk said. There were a few other patrons there, at tables and up at the bar, and Kirk gave a deep sigh of relief. He'd been beginning to wonder if the assassination attempt had the whole city on high alert.

Finnegan came pounding down the sidewalk and through the front doorway of the Warp Core, breathing heavily.

"You really ought to cut down on the potatoes there, Finnegan. How are you ever going to get a girlfriend if you can't run her down?"

Finnegan squeezed his spork so tight, Kirk thought he might snap it in half.

"Ah, ah, ah," Kirk said. He nodded toward the bar. "We've got company. I'm safe."

Finnegan smiled. "That's right, Jimmy boy. For now. But I'm gonna sit right here," he said, pulling out a chair at the table by the door. "And if you try to leave, out the front *or* the back, I'll be on you like fleas on a Varkolak. Garçon! Beer me!"

Kirk hadn't thought about that. Like a kid hugging home in a game of tag in the backyard, he was safe as long as he didn't leave, but he couldn't stay here forever. He looked around the pub, trying to think of an answer, and saw an attractive blonde one sitting at the bar. He put on his most charming smile and pulled up a stool next to her.

"Know what you want?" Bom asked as he came back from delivering Finnegan's beer.

"Yeah. Whaddya got that's already made? I'm starving."

"We've got chili on the stove. You want yellow alert or red alert?"

"Red alert. And two beers—one for me and one for this beautiful lady."

The girl next to him rolled her eyes at him.

"Name's Jim. Jim Kirk," he told her.

"Valerie," she said. Even though she had scoffed at his come on, she accepted the beer with a nod of thanks.

Bom put a steaming bowl of chili and a plate of crackers in front of Kirk. "Hang on, I'll get you a spoon."

Kirk pulled his spork out of his pocket and held it up. "No need. I've got my own."

Valerie laughed. "You carry a spoon around with you all the time?"

"Actually, it's a spork," Kirk said. He scooped a bite of chili into his mouth, then gasped and hyperventilated, trying to cool off his tongue. "Red alert," he squeaked, and he chased the chili with a sip of beer.

"So, you carry a *spork* around with you all the time?" Valerie asked.

"Only lately," Kirk said. Between tentative bites of his red-alert chili, Kirk told the girl all about the Assassination Game and Finnegan, pointing him out over by the door. Finnegan raised his own glass of beer and grinned at Kirk.

"All I need now, see, is for you to leave the bar with

me and take me back to your place, and I'll be safe," Kirk finished.

"I gotta tell you, I've heard a lot of them in my time, but that is the *lamest* pick-up line I have ever heard," the girl told him. "Still, you're kind of cute."

Kirk smiled, tossed some credits on the bar, offered Valerie his arm, and strolled out the front door, waving good-bye to Finnegan as he left.

Later that evening, Spock stood in the Academy observation tower, watching Sol set over the Pacific Ocean. The vista was not dissimilar to watching 40 Eridani A set over the Voroth Sea on Vulcan, but for the oddly discordant blue sky of Earth and not the more aesthetically pleasing orange sky of his home planet. Spock had lived on Earth for years now, was half-human himself, and still there was much about this world that remained foreign and mysterious to him.

The turbolift opened behind him. Nyota Uhura, punctual as always, unlike so many other humans. Another thing Spock did not understand. How was it so difficult for humans to arrive where they were supposed to be at a prescribed time?

"Nyota," Spock said. "I was concerned to hear that you were on the dais when the president's shuttle exploded earlier today."

"Were you?" she asked.

Spock frowned. "Of course. Why should I not be?"

Uhura shrugged. "I don't know. I didn't figure you'd be too upset about it."

"I did not say that I was upset; only that I was concerned."

"Right."

Spock was the first to admit, his understanding of human emotional responses was limited, but he nonetheless felt as though he had done or said something to hurt Cadet Uhura's feelings. It was also his experience that admitting he did not understand how he had been in the wrong often compounded the problem, so he pushed on.

"I am relieved you were relatively unharmed."

"Thanks. Can we get on with it?"

"By all means," Spock told her. Uhura's no-nonsense approach was something else he admired in her—and found lacking in so many other humans.

"I was contacted by the Graviton Society," Uhura told him "I'm in, and they already have a job for me. They want me to steal a Varkolak sniffer."

"Sniffer?"

"One of their scanning devices."

Spock processed this information. The society had no doubt chosen her for this task as she had access to the Varkolak that few other cadets had, and possession of one of the highly advanced sensor units would certainly be a valuable piece of intelligence. It was also significant for another reason.

"This is the first time since my association with the Graviton Society that they have advocated something illegal," he said.

"Not just illegal, Spock, but dangerous. If I'm caught . . ."

"Yes. The interstellar ramifications would be significant."

"That's an understatement," Uhura said.

It was Spock's experience that most humans tended to *over*state matters, but he felt this was not the time to press the point. "I think we must take this request as both evidence of potentially larger, more nefarious activities on the part of the society," he instead told her, "and a measure of your loyalty to the organization."

"You mean, like some sort of initiation test?" Uhura asked.

"Possibly, though this task would seem to be above and beyond the usually frivolous requisites for admittance to less political fraternal organizations. There is also the possibility they are testing your relationship to me."

"Which is what?" Uhura asked.

Spock blinked. "Covert agent to fellow covert agent."

Uhura nodded. "Just checking."

Again, Spock felt as though he had given the wrong answer, even though it had been the most accurate one.

"Will it be possible for you to accede to their request?" he asked her.

"You mean you want me to do it?"

"I acknowledge that the activity is illegal, and potentially dangerous. I only ask if it is possible."

"Maybe. I don't know. I'm supposed to go back with the linguistics team for more face time with the Varkolak, but they protect those sniffer things like they were state secrets."

"As well they should. If you can at least make an attempt, that may satisfy your handler within the society. Should you prove successful, it would solidify your position of trust within the group and potentially open up larger, more important avenues of investigation for us. If nothing else, the ultimate destination of the sniffer, as you call it, could tell us just how high into Starfleet's ranks this organization really goes."

If Spock was any judge of human facial expressions at all, Uhura was still unsure.

"If you were caught in the attempt, Starfleet would of course be made aware of your role in my investigation, and you would be cleared of wrongdoing," he assured her.

"Yeah. But that's not going to go a long way with the Varkolak," Uhura said. "Look, Commander, there's something else. Something I overheard as Dr. Lartal, one of the Varkolak, left the interrogation room today. One of his men asked him, 'Now, how will you kill her?' Or maybe, 'Now, how will you catch her?' It's hard to say. But the reference was definitely from the Varkolak terminology for a hunt, so 'catch' and 'kill' in that sense seem to mean the same thing. Lartal attacked the other man, telling him to be quiet, but he saw me. Spock, he knows I understood every word."

"Then you must abandon the Graviton Society and their request immediately, and recuse yourself from further linguistic studies with the Varkolak."

Uhura looked shocked and, if Spock was "reading" her correctly, almost . . . *pleased* by his words?

"You—you want me to want me to just walk away?" Uhura asked.

"This information drastically changes the situation. Your safety in this endeavor is now a grave concern," he told her.

Uhura stepped closer, and Spock fought back the human, emotional part of him that yearned for her, and the physical part of both halves of him that desired her. "Spock . . . I didn't think you cared."

"I do care," he assured her. "The mission has become untenable."

"The mission," Uhura said. She stepped away. "Don't worry, Commander. I can take care of myself."

Uhura went to the turbolift and left without saying good-bye, which Spock knew was odd behavior for a human. Again, he assumed he had done or said something to offend her, but he had no idea what.

Spock looked back out the window at the now pink and orange yet incongruously sunless sky and wondered again at this world that remained so foreign and mysterious.

CH.10.30
House Calls

Leonard McCoy staggered back to his dorm room like a man coming home from a three-day bender. After ten straight hours of triage, he could barely hold himself up. The exploding shuttle had knocked him unconscious and blown him ten meters off the dais, but after he'd come to his senses, he'd dived in to start treating the wounded. It had been chaos there and in the Academy hospital, where everyone had been taken for treatment. There were dozens of people with lacerations, broken limbs, and burns, not to mention every visiting doctor from thirty-four sectors and two quadrants crowding the ER to lend a hand. But there were no fatalities, thank goodness. Even the president of the Federation had mostly escaped harm, though she'd been whisked away to some other more protected medical facility. At least that meant they hadn't been tripping over presidential security guards too.

He could barely utter his name clearly enough for his door to recognize him, but finally he got into his room. Kirk wasn't there, which probably meant he was spending the night somewhere else again. McCoy was grateful for the quiet. He collapsed facedown onto his bed, still fully-clothed. Tomorrow, bright and early, he and the rest of the medical cadets would be back in the lab, sifting through the thousands of shuttle fragments for DNA evidence. But for now, McCoy could at last enjoy a peaceful, blissful night's sleep. . . .

● · ·   ✦ · ·   ✦   · ✦ · ·

There were dozens of them. Hundreds. More patients than he could possibly hope to take care of. They had gashes on their arms and legs, burns on their chests, broken bones, internal bleeding, head trauma. McCoy rushed from biobed to biobed, doing what he could, calling for help, but he was the only person there. No nurses, no other doctors, no one but an endless stream of patients—Humans, Bolians, Andorians, Vulcans, Ktarians, Denobulans, Trill, Mizarians, Rigelians. They kept coming and coming and coming, all of them in pain, all of them crying out for him to help them. But he just . . . couldn't . . . get to them all in time.

The door chime sounded, and McCoy called for

whomever it was to come in. Heaven knew he could use the help.

The door chime rang again. And again. And again.

"Come in! Come in, damn it! I can't come to the door!" McCoy cried, rushing to the next patient.

The door chimed again, and McCoy jerked awake. Where was he? What time was it? He was on his bed, in his uniform, and it was pitch-black in the room. He dragged his alarm clock over to him, knocking an empty glass to the floor with a thud. 0226. His alarm wasn't set to go off for another two and half hours. He'd been having an awful dream, about an ER with a neverending stream of patients—

The door chime rang yet again. For real this time. McCoy dragged himself out of bed and lurched to the door. He pushed the admit button, and the door slid open onto a brightly lit hallway that made him wince. But no one was there. He leaned out the door to squint up and down the hall. Still nobody.

The door chime went off again. No, wait. Not the door chime. His half-asleep brain was starting to work again, and he realized it wasn't the door chime at all. It was the sound of his communicator. He closed the door against the awful light and fumbled around for his satchel. Found his communicator and pulled it out. Someone had been trying to call him for fifteen minutes. Who the devil called at two thirty in the morning? He glanced at Jim's empty bed. If this was Kirk and he wasn't missing an arm or a leg, he soon would be. McCoy flipped his communicator open.

"Who the hell calls at two thirty in the—"

"Priority One call from Nadja Luther," said a recorded voice.

"Leonard? Leonard, it's Nadja."

Weariness drained from McCoy and he stood up straighter. "Nadja? What's wrong? Why are you calling—"

"Leonard, I need you to meet me at Cavallo Point, right away," Nadja said.

"What? Now? Why?"

"Please, hurry," Nadja said.

"Nadja? What's wrong? Nadja?" McCoy said.

"Priority One call ended," the computer voice said again, and his communicator went silent. McCoy immediately tried calling her back, but there was no answer. He replayed the conversation again; the whole thing automatically recorded as a Priority One call. There was such urgency in her voice. Such panic.

McCoy grabbed his satchel and charged out into the bright hallway. He tried Nadja again, and when he got no answer again, he picked up his pace. Cavallo Point was a public area out past the marina on San Francisco Bay. Ordinarily he would have taken a ground shuttle, but they weren't running this late at night. The only people around as he hurried from Yi Sun-Sin Hall were the Academy's few nocturnal students, going to and from class. One of them gave him a second look as he hurried past. McCoy realized he must have looked like death warmed over.

He hurried across the old parade grounds and past the Academy administration buildings, where only the exterior illumination lights were on. He didn't see a soul as he reached Sommerville Road and hurried down past the marina and up to Cavallo Point. He was so tired, he felt like he was running the Academy marathon, an event he had absolutely zero interest in participating in. He reached the point at last, stopping just long enough to put his hands on his knees and catch his breath.

"Nadja?" he called. "Nadja? It's Leonard! Leonard McCoy!"

Of course it's Leonard McCoy, he chided himself. How many other Leonards does she know? But he was tired and worried, so he cut himself some slack.

"Nadja? Nadja?" he tried again. No answer. He was starting to really worry. He tried her communicator again and got no answer again—nor did he hear it ringing anywhere nearby.

After a cursory search of the small area illuminated by street lights, McCoy decided it was no use. She wasn't here—or if she was, he couldn't locate her. It was time to bring in some help, he realized.

"Academy Security," he told his communicator, and he cursed with frustration as he waited for them to pick up.

"Cadet Luther? Cadet Luther, are you there? Campus security. Please open up."

McCoy stood behind the female security officer, twitching impatiently. "I'm telling you, this is a waste of time," he told the officer. "She called me from Cavallo Point and told me—"

Nadja's door slid open, and there she stood in a T-shirt that just covered her. Her hair was a rumpled mess, and she blinked sleepily in the light from the hallway. "Hello? Yes? Leonard? Is that you?"

"I'm sorry to disturb you, miss," the officer said. "But we had a report that you were missing." She held up a tricorder to verify that this was, in fact, Cadet Luther, and seemed satisfied with the results.

"Missing? Who said I was missing?"

"I did!" McCoy told her. He stepped around the security officer and held up his communicator. "You called me. Told me to come out to Cavallo Point. When I got there, you weren't there."

"Cavallo Point?" She squinted in the light. "I wasn't at Cavallo Point. I was here. Asleep."

"Dr. McCoy," the officer said, "The campus is on high alert after the bombing of the president's shuttle. This is *not* the time to be using Academy Security as your personal dating service when a girl won't answer your calls."

"Now wait just a cotton-pickin' minute!" McCoy started. "You don't think I—"

Nadja winced and put a hand up to stop the noisy argument. "My communicator's missing. It's been missing since this morning."

"Did you report this, miss?" the officer asked.

Nadja nodded. "To the Cochrane Hall staff, yes. I think that's where I lost it."

"Your communicator's missing?" McCoy asked. "But someone called me using your voice! How could they do that? And *why* would they do that?"

"All right. If everyone's fine here, I'm going to check back in," the security officer said. She shot McCoy a suspicious look and went away.

"Great. Now campus security thinks I'm using them to make booty calls. *Which I'm not,*" he added hastily.

Nadja smirked. "Well, since you're here now, and we're both up . . . Would you like to come in?"

"No," McCoy said. "I mean, yes, but no. I've got to be in the lab first thing, and I need to get back to sleep. But I'd like to see you again soon. How about dinner, tomorrow night?"

"All right. It's a date." Nadja gave McCoy a kiss. "And

thanks for coming to my rescue, even if I didn't need rescuing."

McCoy's lack of sleep caught up with him again on the walk back to his dorm as the adrenaline rush of the night wore off. His head was still full of questions: Who had Nadja's communicator? Why had they called him to Cavallo Point? How had they imitated her voice? What was this about?

All of that would have to wait. He mumbled his name to his dorm room door and stumbled inside again, feeling a profound sense of déjà vu. He dropped his satchel to the floor and fell face-first onto his bed. He was just slipping into a glorious, blissful sleep when his alarm went off.

It was time to get ready for class.

CH.11.30
Sparring Partners

Martial arts were part of The Plan.

Hikaru Sulu rose early every morning to go through his karate routine at the Academy Sports Complex before classes. Every cadet was required to take some form of self-defense class, but not everyone devoted time to the practice outside of class. Sulu had been doing karate since he was a boy, though, and he not only thought of his time in the gym as dedication to his studies, but also as time to arrange his thoughts and prepare for the coming day. Pavel Chekov, the cadet who kept trying to get him to do something together in their free time, had said the same thing once about his running, though Sulu wondered how Chekov ever reigned in that overactive brain of his.

Usually, Sulu would go through his daily schedule, ordering the work he still needed to do for each class by priority. But not today. His shoulder and wrist still ached from yesterday's explosion, and he found himself slowing and pulling his punches, which took him out of the rhythm of his workout. But there was something else on his mind besides his classes.

Today he was supposed to carry out a mission for the Graviton Society.

Sulu struck the practice pole's pads, working from head to toe in sequence as best as he could. Doing a job for the Graviton Society was definitely not part of The Plan. But for better or worse, he'd made his decision, and once a course correction was laid in, it *became* the new course. The old course was now nothing more than a navigation log entry. Something in the past. He had a new target, a new destination, and now that he was committed, he needed to stay focused on that course and no other.

Sulu rattled the karate pole with a kick and came set again, sparing a moment for a glance around the sports complex. *She* came here every morning to work out too, though not exclusively to work on her martial arts. She varied her regimen, he'd noted, sometimes running the track, sometimes working the rings, other times practicing Suus Mahna. Yesterday she'd put in a particularly long session practicing the Vulcan martial art, giving her *rofarla* dummy quite a beating.

There. Cadet Uhura was limbering up before her morning exercise. Sulu struck the pole and tried not to stare.

His mission was to pass along information to Uhura—false information—with the expectation that if she were a mole, it would be passed along to Commander Spock. Then if Starfleet Security acted on the information, the Graviton Society would know Spock was passing along their secrets and that Cadet Uhura had been brought into the fold to give the Vulcan commander another pair of ears and eyes within the organization. If the information didn't pass up the ranks to Starfleet . . . Well, at least Cadet Uhura would be in the clear.

Sulu glanced Uhura's way again as she jogged out onto the indoor track. So it was to be laps this morning. That was disappointing. Now he'd have to hope that Suus Mahna practice would be a part of her later routine and that she didn't compensate for yesterday's zealousness by skipping it altogether.

He was just contemplating trying to run the track with her and engage Uhura there when the scattered conversations and clink of weight training around the complex died and the big gym became silent. Sulu turned to where everyone else was looking and stared with them: coming into the sports complex together were an Academy cadet, one of the Varkolak, and a virtual battalion of Starfleet Security officers. The cadet Sulu didn't know, but he'd seen him around campus, wagging his tongue and batting his eyes at every female cadet from Andoria to Zakdorn. But what on earth was he doing here now, with a Varkolak?

The entourage disappeared into the men's changing rooms, and conversations began around the gym. Angry conversations. Most people thought the Varkolak were behind yesterday's shuttle explosion, and Sulu happened to agree with them. There couldn't have been any proof, though, or Starfleet wouldn't be letting the Varkolak out of their compound. That would also explain why Sulu and every other cadet were being scanned and logged whenever they left their dorms and whenever they entered a building on campus. Everyone was a suspect.

The Casanova cadet and the Varkolak emerged from the changing room a little while later wearing Velocity uniforms and headed for the Velocity courts on the north side of the complex. Their security escorts still wore their Starfleet uniforms, of course. The animated chatter in the gymnasium died down again, and no one bothered to hide the fact that they were staring at the Varkolak as he and the cadet left the room. Sulu didn't know what that was all about, but it didn't matter. He had a job to do before class.

He glanced again at the track, but Uhura was gone. His eyes went to the gymnastics area, but she wasn't there. She wasn't in the martial-arts training area, either. Damn. Had she already left? But she usually spent a good forty-five to fifty minutes in the sports complex each morning. She couldn't be finished already. . . .

No. There she was. She hadn't left yet, but she was heading for the changing rooms. Sulu broke away from his practice dummy and jogged to catch up with her as nonchalantly as possible. Unless he ran, he wasn't going to reach her before she made it to the women's dressing rooms. But then, unexpectedly, she made a course correction and headed for the men's changing rooms. She glanced back over her shoulder to see if anyone was watching her, and Sulu quickly averted his eyes and pretended to be very interested in two cadets who were wrestling. When he looked back, Uhura was slipping into the open entrance to the men's dressing rooms. What was she up to?

Sulu's natural inclination was to peel away, to let her do whatever it was she meant to do without confronting her or engaging her, but that was the old course.

This was a new heading.

"Cadet Uhura!" he called. She visibly jumped, spinning around to face him as he caught up to her. Her face was flushed and her eyes were wide. "Cadet Uhura," Sulu said again. "I think you've got the wrong changing room." He pointed helpfully to the sign that read MEN in ten different Federation languages and carried the interplanetary symbol for the male sex.

"Oh!" Uhura said. "I didn't—I don't know where my head was." She quickly moved away from the entrance to the men's changing room.

"Maybe you thought it was the neutral changing room?" Sulu said. "It's just across the gym—"

"No. I just—I just wasn't thinking, I guess. Autopilot, you know?"

It had to be unintentional, he knew, but Sulu grinned at the helm reference.

"Your name is . . . Sulu, isn't it?" Uhura said, and now it was Sulu's turn to blush. He didn't think she knew he existed.

"Hikaru Sulu," he said, giving her a slight bow.

"I've seen you practicing, what is it, karate?" she said. "You're very good."

"It's nothing," Sulu said. "Would you like to spar with me?"

Sulu tried not to close his eyes in embarrassment. He'd planned on making that invitation a little more smoothly. That one was more like trying to go to warp with the external inertial dampeners on.

"I—oh," Uhura said. A passing instructor gave her a look as he went into the men's changing rooms, and Uhura took Sulu's arm and dragged him away. "Yes."

Sulu was a bit stunned at his success, but tried not to show it. Whatever Uhura had needed or wanted in the changing rooms, she didn't seem to care now. Together they found a place on the martial arts mats and took up their positions.

"Suus Mahna," Sulu said, identifying her fighting style.

"I haven't been practicing it for very long," Uhura said.

"You'll have to go easy on me." They circled each other warily. "How long have you been taking karate?"

Sulu moved in for a strike. She blocked most of it, but not the sweeping leg that sent her to the mat.

"All my life," he told her. He offered her a hand and pulled her back up. "Do you want to stop?"

"No, no," she said. She had a harder look in her eyes now, one that said she wasn't about to give up. Sulu had seen that look before. In the mirror.

"I've seen you practicing before," Uhura said, "but you never spar with anyone." She led with an elbow, and he blocked it instinctively, forgetting his injured wrist. He grimaced as it gave, and was too slow trying to stop her from twisting his arm. She flipped him to the mat and stood over him, smiling. "Do you want to stop?"

"No," Sulu said, acknowledging the repeat of his own question with a smile. "It looks like I'll have to keep my *shields up.*"

The words had the effect he'd anticipated. Uhura's smile faltered.

"Right about now, you're probably wondering if that was just a casual metaphor or something with a little more . . . gravity," he told her as he stood.

"I'm assuming it's the latter, then," she said. He had her attention now for sure. "Were you one of them the other night? In the robes?"

Sulu hadn't been at whatever meeting she was talking about, but if it was anything like the night he'd been invited . . . There was a room full of hooded and robed people he hadn't been able to identify. If he told her he was there, she'd never know he wasn't.

"Yes," he lied. "Welcome to the society."

They sparred again, this time neither of them going to the mat. Sulu protected his wrist, limiting his movement, but compensated for it with his feet. When they had fought to a standstill, they backed away for a breather. Sulu glanced at the clock on the sports complex wall. It was almost 0700 hours. He was going to miss his first class of the day. Sulu never missed class. His mother certainly hadn't allowed it when he was a boy, no matter how sick he was or whatever else might be happening in their lives, and he'd never missed a university class or an Academy class once he'd been out on his own. He had stayed on course his entire life, only to change headings here, now, at the last moment.

Stay on target, he told himself.

"So, are you part of this Graviton plan to torture the Varkolak into leaving?" Sulu asked.

The question distracted her, and he scored a hit. To her credit, Uhura recovered nicely, using a *Po grot ma* defense. Sulu pulled back and didn't press his attack, letting her regain her feet and consider her next plan of attack.

"Yes," Uhura told him. "But I still don't understand how Starfleet Security isn't going to catch wind of it."

Sulu smiled inwardly. Uhura had taken the bait, just as Daagen expected her to. Uhura couldn't be a part of the Graviton plan to drive the Varkolak away because there *was* no plan to drive them off Earth. Not one Sulu knew about, anyway. But if Starfleet Security moved against this fictional one . . .

"The engineers say no one will be able to hear the high-frequency signal except the Varkolak. And any other dogs on campus, of course. Admiral Archer's beagle will probably be howling for days, poor thing. They say they can mask the broadcast location, but who's going to think the signal is being broadcast from the Academy's own communication tower?"

"Right," Uhura said, her mind on the plot, not the fight. Sulu feinted low, then attacked high, knocking Uhura off balance. Sulu threw her on her back, and she hit the mat with a thud.

Sulu offered Uhura his hand. "But at least we know they're not going to hear it from us."

"The game," said Kirk, "is called Velocity."

He activated the Velocity panel, and a spinning disk emerged from a slot in the wall and hovered in front of them.

Lartal sniffed at the thing with his long snout. "What does it do?"

"Well, it kind of just . . . spins there. Until you shoot it."

Kirk and Lartal were the only two people in the small room. Their Starfleet Security escorts stood outside the only door to the Velocity court, which was closed so that it became a seamless part of the wall. Bones had suggested Kirk do something with Lartal that *he* liked to do, and Kirk immediately thought of Velocity. He had other reasons too.

Kirk pulled a phaser from a compartment in the wall and activated it. He'd never played Velocity until he came to the Academy—not too many gyms in Iowa had the facilities for a game that used live phasers—but he'd taken to it immediately. A game where you fired phasers at targets and ducked and rolled, avoiding obstacles? Starfleet Academy called it away team training. Kirk called it the best game ever invented.

Kirk shot the spinning disk with his phaser, and it changed color.

Lartal was unimpressed. "Is that all it does? Change color?"

"No. I've got the safeties on now." Kirk shot the disk again. It changed color again, and spun faster. He shot it again, and again it changed color and spun even faster. "When the safeties are off, the disk flies around the room.

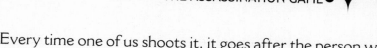

Every time one of us shoots it, it goes after the person with the other phaser, faster and faster, until one of us isn't quick enough and gets tagged."

Kirk disengaged the safeties, and the Velocity disk came flying at him. He shot it, knocking it away, only to have it come back at him faster. He ducked, rolled, shot it again. It kicked away and returned, faster. He fired, hitting it, and rolled back to where he had begun. He hopped up and tapped the safety on the console, stopping the spinning disk mere inches from his head.

"That was single-player mode," Kirk said. He pulled a second phaser from the wall compartment and put it in Lartal's hand.

The Varkolak raised an eyebrow, and Kirk laughed inwardly. Some expressions transcended race and space.

"You are giving me a Federation type-2 phase pistol?" Lartal said. While the Varkolak had the most advanced sensing equipment by far of anyone the Federation had yet come into contact with, their phaser technology reportedly lagged behind Starfleet's.

"Let's just consider that a loan, shall we?" Kirk said. "And you'll note the kill setting is disabled on all game weapons."

Lartal flicked the switch on the phaser that made the blue stun setting rotate to the red kill setting, pointed the pistol at Kirk, and squeezed the trigger. Nothing happened, and Kirk didn't flinch.

"Just checking," Lartal said. He grinned his wolfy grin and flipped the phaser setting back to stun. "Every Varkolak captain in the armada would give his right paw for one of these."

"Trade you one for that tricorder of yours," Kirk told him.

Lartal howled with laughter. "An intriguing offer! But one that might get us both torn to pieces for treason."

"Well, we don't tear one another to pieces, but it would be something just as bad, yeah," Kirk said. "What do you say? You want to try it?"

"By all means," Lartal said.

Kirk knew he wouldn't be able to resist. Lartal was more Kirk than Bones. More command officer than medical officer. Kirk nodded and reset the Velocity disk.

"Game on," Kirk said.

The disk hummed around the room. Kirk shot first, changing the disk from violet to indigo. The Velocity disk recoiled, then came at Lartal.

"You intrigue me, Kirk," Lartal said. He shot and missed the disk as he got a feel for the phaser. It came after him, still slow at this stage of the game, and Lartal adjusted his aim and fired again, striking it. "Your friends in the hall, all the cadets in the gym—they seem to have tried and convicted me for yesterday's bombing."

The disk changed from indigo to blue and did a circle of the room, homing in on Kirk.

"Well, I'm still not sure I buy the fact that your scanning device told you that shuttle was about to blow up," Kirk said. He dodged the Velocity disk and shot it as it passed. "But was it my imagination, or did you knock me out of the way of that explosion?"

The disk turned green and got faster. This was the level of the game that began to separate the pros from the amateurs. The command officers from the medical officers.

"You humans are known for weak-minded fantasies. It was no doubt your imagination."

Lartal rolled and came up firing. A hit. The disk changed from green to yellow and sped at Kirk. His first shot missed as he threw himself out of the way, but he crossed his body with his next shot and tagged the disk. It changed to orange and circled the room almost too fast to keep up with. If Lartal shot it out of the air, it would fly at Kirk at its highest speed, catching him before he could get back to his feet.

Lartal sprinted around the room, dodging, ducking, rolling, twisting out of the disk's way, but for some reason he didn't shoot at it. The Varkolak's delay gave Kirk just enough time to get up. The moment he was on his feet, Lartal hit the disk square on. A direct hit, on the highest and hardest level of Velocity.

Definitely not the marksmanship of a doctor.

It was the last thing Kirk thought before the Velocity disk came screaming at his head.

CH.12.30
Circumstantial Evidence

McCoy dragged himself into the medical lab with the rest of the medical cadets, wishing the security officers outside hadn't made him pour out his coffee. No outside liquids were allowed into secure facilities now. Preposterous! A simple phoretic scan could have cleared his coffee and allowed him to self-medicate with caffeine, but the scanner hadn't passed peer review yet. He went to his carrel and put his head down on the desk instead, hoping to catch just a few more seconds' rest before the instructors put them to work sifting through the debris from the shuttle explosion.

"I wondered how you could sleep knowing that foolish idealism like yours allowed the Federation's worst enemies into our own backyard, and now I see that you can't," said a familiar voice.

Lifting his head felt like waking from anesthesia, but McCoy looked up.

"Cadet Daagen," McCoy said. "Go jump in a lake."

The Tellarite frowned. "Does this expression have some metaphorical meaning on Earth besides its literal one?"

McCoy put his head back down on the desk. "Yes. It means go the hell away."

Something clattered to the desk beside McCoy.

"Here. You can give this back to your equally foolish girlfriend. I found it on my desk this morning."

McCoy's eyelid fluttered open, and what he saw woke him up faster than a hypospray full of cortalin. It was a communicator. *Nadja's* communicator.

"Found this on your desk? That's a load of hooey, and you know it!" McCoy said. He stood and glared down at the diminutive Tellarite. "What's the big idea, Daagen, prank calling me at two thirty in the morning, pretending to be Nadja, sending me on some damned fool snipe hunt!"

"I don't know what you're talking about," Daagen said.

"The hell you don't!" McCoy punched up the call log on the communicator. "Look here. This is where somebody called my phone at two twenty-six in the morning. Maybe you can explain to me how somebody used this phone to call me when it was sitting on *your* desk all night."

"I can't explain it, because I didn't call you."

"Cadets, if I can have your attention," a Starfleet Medical officer called from the front of the room. "We're going to begin bringing in the debris samples in just a moment. If you could each return to your carrels, we'll bring you a tray to analyze. Please run the usual tests: electron resonance scanner, molecular scanner, biocomputer. The Starfleet Corps of Engineers will run mass spectrometer readings and other tests to check for explosive particulates when we're finished, but what we're looking for is anything biological that will give us a clue to the perpetrator."

Daagen turned to leave, but McCoy caught him by the arm. "I don't know what you're up to, Daagen, but it's not funny."

The Tellarite yanked his arm away and went to his seat. Prank calling someone you didn't like was nothing new, but McCoy didn't see what was so funny about this one.

A security officer set a tray of metal fragments in front of him, and McCoy put the first of the pieces in the molecular scanner. The duranium was twisted and scarred from the blast, and it brought back, vividly, the horror of the moment when McCoy had been caught in the blast. If Daagen's little stunt hadn't woken him up, reliving the explosion certainly would have.

McCoy put the piece through the rest of the standard medical scanners, but there was nothing unusual about it. He was about to set it aside and move on to the next piece when he had the idea to run the specimen through the experimental phoretic analyzer he'd been testing for Dr. Huer. It certainly wouldn't hurt anything, and if it turned up something useful . . . Well, they'd have to confirm it with an independent analysis. But in a case like this, the sooner they could get a lead on something, the better.

The phoretic analyzer scanned the debris, then flashed and hummed as it processed the individual molecules. Most of it would be duranium, with a little carbon thrown in from the scoring, and random particulates from wherever the piece had landed. What McCoy hadn't expected to find made him call a medical officer over right away. A Starfleet Security officer joined him.

"What is it, Cadet?" the officer asked. Cadets peeked over the tops of their carrels, curious to see what McCoy had found too.

"Kemocite," McCoy said.

"Kemocite? That's a radiolytic compound, isn't it? What kind of medical scan turned up kemocite?"

"The engineering teams would have turned it up with a mass spectrometer, but the phoretic analyzer found it when I was scanning for biological molecules." McCoy explained the phoretic analyzer to the officers, and they reviewed his results.

"I still don't understand," the medical officer said. "How does this help?"

"Kemocite's a power source," the security officer told him.

"Yeah," said McCoy. "The same power source the Varkolak use in all their technology."

The medical lab buzzed with this new development, but the officers in charge quickly got everyone back to work. The kemocite discovery was damning, McCoy knew, but nowhere near conclusive. Kemocite could be had most anywhere. Hell, the Academy engineering lab probably had a kilo of the stuff in storage.

McCoy's communicator rang, and he stepped outside to take the call.

"Bones! Bones, am I glad you picked up." It was Jim Kirk, of course.

"Yeah, look, I'm kind of in the middle of something here, Jim."

"Whatever it is, you've got to drop it and get over here right away. Academy Sports Complex."

"Jim, it took me thirty minutes to get through all this new security, just to get inside the damn medical building. I can't just pop over for a game of Parrises Square."

"Bones, it's an emergency. I wouldn't call you if it wasn't important."

McCoy looked back through the glass wall at the cadets running scans on the shuttle fragments. He hated to bail on something that could help solve the mystery of the explosion, but it was really nothing more than putting debris under an electron resonance scanner and pushing a button. There were plenty of cadets to do the job. And this was Jim asking.

"All right. I'll be there."

Kirk waited just inside the doorway to the Academy Sports Complex, watching the sidewalk outside. The security officers at the entrance watched Kirk. He smiled lamely and waved. After the assassination attempt on the president, just standing around looked suspicious. One of the security officers had just started to approach him when Bones hurried in, a portable medical kit in his hand. Kirk went outside to meet him.

"Where does it hurt? What's happened?" Bones asked.

The security officers stopped him to scan and log him in.

"Damn it, people, I've got a medical emergency here," Bones griped. They had barely finished scanning him when he pushed ahead, medical tricorder in hand and already on. "You've got a minor contusion on your forehead, Jim, but it's nothing serious. You were right to call me, though. Head injuries are nothing to mess around with."

Kirk pulled Bones out of earshot of the security officers. "No, no. That's not why I called," he told his friend. He glanced back over his shoulder. "I need you to walk me

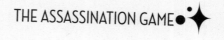

back to the dorm. Finnegan could be lying in wait for me anywhere."

Kirk could practically see the blood rising in Bones's face, like in some cartoon.

"You called me away from scanning debris from the explosion so I could play chaperone for you in some stupid game? Jim, of all the absolutely ridiculous—"

"You were scanning the debris?" Kirk asked, trying to change the subject. It was easy—and fun, too—to get Bones riled up, but it was just as easy to get him distracted. Anything about his work would do. "Did you find anything?"

"Yes, damn it, I did," Bones said. His anger ebbed away as he shifted gears to medical mode, just as Kirk had predicted. "Jim, listen. I found traces of kemocite on some of the debris."

Kirk waved Bones quiet as they made their way back through security, then picked up the conversation again on the way back to the dorm.

"Kemocite? Vent plasma from a shuttle's engines and add kemocite to it and . . ."

"Boom," Bones said. "Yeah. And you know who uses kemocite to power all their gadgets."

"The Varkolak," Kirk said. "I know. I just don't get it."

"Get what?"

"Lartal, this Varkolak. Bones, I don't think he's a

doctor . . . but I don't think he's behind all this, either. I know he dove away from the explosion milliseconds before it went off, but he took me with him. Bones, he knocked me to the ground. To protect me. I'm sure of it. Why would someone set a bomb and then make sure no one got hurt by it?"

"Maybe he didn't set it," Bones said. "Maybe it was one of the other Varkolak."

Kirk shook his head. "No. Lartal's not a doctor. He's a command officer of some kind. I'm sure of it. Unless you know any doctors who can reach red level on Velocity. And win."

"Hell, I can't get past indigo," Bones said. "Is that where you got the bump on your noggin? You mean, he *beat* you? Jim, I thought you hadn't lost a Velocity match since you got here."

"I lost this one. On purpose. I took a dive, Bones." Kirk stopped. "I let the Velocity disk tag me and played dead. Or unconscious, anyway."

"What on Earth for?"

"I wanted to see if Lartal would try to steal one of the phasers."

Bones scoffed. "You can't take Velocity phasers out of the arena. The alarm would go off."

"Yeah, *I* know that, and *you* know that, but Lartal doesn't know that. He could have hidden one inside his uniform and tried to walk out with it. But he didn't, Bones. He didn't even try to take the thing apart. He just sat there with me and waited for me to wake up."

"Maybe he knew you were faking it."

"Maybe. I don't know. Bones, I'm telling you, I don't think bombing a shuttle is these guys' MO. When we were playing Velocity, I could swear Lartal gave me a chance to get to my feet before he sent the disk after me. It's like they've got some code of honor or something."

"Well, they're looking for DNA evidence right now to see if they can corroborate the kemocite traces. Which is what *I* should be doing, not playing nursemaid to—"

"Bones, are you all right?" Kirk asked, trying to change the subject again. "You look like hell. Have you been getting enough sleep?"

"No, damn it, I haven't. That's another thing. Last night, at two thirty in the morning, I got a call from Nadja."

Kirk raised the old eyebrows. "Hot and heavy house call?"

"Hardly," Bones groused. He explained everything that had happened last night as they walked. "And then, this morning, this medical cadet, Daagen—one of those 'Federation First' idiots—hands me her communicator and tells me he just 'found' it on his desk."

"He prank called you? But it's not Dead Week." Dead Week was the week of pranks and insanity that usually happened right around finals time, when cadets needed to blow off some steam.

"No. And it's not funny. He says he didn't do it, but for cryin' out loud, Jim. Who else would do it? And why?"

"And why go to all that trouble?" Kirk asked.

"Listen, Jim . . . I know this is going to sound crazy, but what if Daagen is up to something? Something more serious?"

"What do you mean?"

"I mean, like, what if he and his 'Federation First' buddies pulled that stunt at the opening ceremonies and are trying to pin the blame on the Varkolak?"

Kirk couldn't believe what he was hearing. "A *cadet*? Someone from Starfleet? I just can't believe that. We take an *oath*, Bones—"

"I know, I know. But some people may believe in that a little more than others."

"Still. There's no way. I don't know who was behind it, but I refuse to believe it was someone in Starfleet."

"You're too trusting, Jim."

"I have to be, Bones. Otherwise, what's the point? So, what's next for you and Nadja? Got a hot date lined up?"

"Jim, we're talking about a terrorist bombing here, and you want to know how my love life's going?"

"I have to, Bones," Kirk said. "Otherwise, what's the point?" He grinned. "Come on. You've been thinking about it too. I know you have. Spill."

"All right. Yes. I do have something lined up. I'm taking your advice and we're going out for dinner under the stars."

Kirk tapped Bones on the shoulder with his fist. "There we go! I knew you had it in you. So, where is it? Somewhere in the city?"

"No, it's a little farther out than that. I had this idea. I'm going to—"

"Sounds great, Bones," Kirk told him. He'd just spotted Cadet Rhinehart walking alone toward the cafeteria. He was Kirk's next target in the Assassination Game. He took off at a run, trying to catch him before he got company. "Thanks for the escort. See you back in the dorm!"

"Glad I could miss out on important lab work to be your babysitter!" he heard Bones call out from behind him. "You owe me, Jim!"

CH.13.30
Date Night

The Academy Observation Tower was bright and sun-filled when Uhura stepped off the turbolift that day at lunch. Ordinarily, the added sight of Spock waiting there by the window would have made the picture more perfect, but now he stood like a dark cloud on her horizon. She would tell him her news as quickly as possible, she told herself, and maybe that way stay out of the rain.

"Nyota," Spock said.

"Commander Spock."

Spock heard the formality in her voice, but did nothing more than raise an eyebrow, damn him. Whatever.

"Have you had an opportunity to acquire one of the Varkolak sensing devices?" Spock asked her.

"No. I mean, yes, I had an opportunity, but it didn't work out." She told Spock about the Varkolak who had visited the Academy Sports Complex that morning and her attempt to sneak into the men's changing rooms to steal his scanner. That elicited another raised eyebrow from him, but nothing more.

"I was interrupted by a cadet named Hikaru Sulu. Do you know him?"

"I am acquainted with him, yes. From my work with the Academy simulators. He is an able pilot."

Uhura rubbed her sore neck. "He's also good at karate too. *And* he's a member of the Graviton Society."

"Is he?"

"He approached me this morning. Asked me to spar with him. While we were fighting, he let it slip that the Gravitons are planning to get rid of the Varkolak."

"Indeed?"

Uhura laid out the plot for him. "You'll have to tell Starfleet Security. They can post extra guards on the communications tower."

"I will take care of it, thank you."

"So. Okay, then," Uhura said. There was really nothing more to say. "I'm going to get some lunch before my next class."

Spock moved to one side to reveal two cartons of Chinese food from a restaurant just off campus. "I took the liberty of procuring two orders of kung pao vegetables. Your favorite, if I am not mistaken. I thought we might eat lunch together."

Uhura was stunned. "You mean . . . like a date?"

Spock frowned. "I merely meant to offer sustenance,

as I have imposed upon your scheduled lunch hour. And as we should not be seen together during this operation, dining together in the faculty cafeteria or the student dining hall is inadvisable."

"Right," Uhura said. "I uh, I appreciate the offer, but I have other plans."

"I understand," Spock told her as she walked to the turbolift, but she doubted he did.

● · ·✦ ·: ✦ · ✦ ·· ·

"Ready for our big date?"

Nadja Luther looked ready. She was wearing a low-cut, sleeveless dress that hugged her slight body—nothing too fancy, but not too casual either—and had her long dark hair done up on top of her head. McCoy caught the dull shine of something metal holding her hair in place, and shook his head.

"Don't tell me—that's a spork."

Nadja slipped her arm in his. "Well, you never know who you're going to end up alone with, do you?"

"Well, I hope you've got it narrowed down, at least."

Nadja flashed him her beautiful smile, and McCoy felt an onset of what he might have diagnosed as presyncope, the light-headedness that preceded a fainting spell, though his symptoms were no doubt psychological, brought about by hyperventilation. In layman's terms,

Nadja was currently working some serious mojo on him.

"So. 'An evening under the stars,'" Nadja said. "Does that mean a night picnic? A fancy dinner under twinkling lights? A hidden garret under the stage at Madame Tussauds in Hollywood?"

"You'll see," McCoy said. He wanted to keep it mysterious. He'd put a lot of planning into this.

McCoy escorted Nadja across campus, but instead of heading for the streetcar line into Sausalito or the ferry landing to take them across the bay to San Francisco, he led her to one of the Academy's transporter rooms.

"Curiouser and curiouser," she told him.

McCoy nodded to the transporter chief on duty. "Two to beam up," he told her.

"Up?" Nadja asked. But before McCoy could even smile in response, they were caught in the snowy white swirl of the transporter beam and broken down into subatomic particles, only to be reassembled moments later on the transporter pad of a fancy restaurant on an orbiting space station.

McCoy took a deep breath and tried not to reel. He hated transporters, but this gag was the only way to get them where he wanted to go. Not without booking a shuttle—and a pilot to go with it.

"Ahh," Nadja said. "So that was your plan." She started to step off the transporter pad, but McCoy held her back.

"Two to beam up," he told the tuxedoed maître d'.

Nadja stared at him now, absolutely flummoxed. Good. An early point for him.

McCoy closed his eyes as they were once more fragmented into billions of particles and transmitted across the vacuum of space, defragmenting on the transporter pad of the USS *Potemkin*. He swayed again, barely resisting the urge to pat himself down for missing parts.

The stupid things men do for love, McCoy thought.

"We're eating on a starship?" Nadja said. McCoy could tell she was impressed. Most cadets never saw a real Starfleet vessel until the annual Zeta Fleet Training Exercise or the USS *Eagle* training run to Alpha Centauri and back. McCoy had interned with Tom Arnet, the *Potemkin*'s doctor, last summer, though, and he'd worked a favor from him while the *Potemkin* was home in the Sol system.

"Ah, ah, ah," McCoy said when Nadja tried to step down, and he held her back once again. Now she didn't look mystified or flummoxed so much as crafty, trying to work out the puzzle of where they were going before they got there. McCoy didn't wait to give her the chance.

"Lieutenant Nguyen, two to beam up, please," McCoy said.

"Abra . . . cadabra," the *Potemkin*'s transporter chief said. If there was one thing McCoy hated, it was

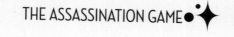

transporter chiefs who tried to be cute. But before he could complain, they were swept up in the white whirlwind one last time and deposited at their final destination.

"The Argos telescope!" Nadja said, and she burst out laughing.

Laughter was all right. It was something of a joke to bring her here, after all. It was the one place every cadet tried so desperately to *avoid*. The assignment was paralyzingly dull, boring, and tedious.

McCoy, of course, had plans to make it otherwise.

He offered Nadja his arm. "I swapped duties with Cadet Morrow. You wouldn't believe how easy it was."

"I can't imagine," Nadja said, all smiles now.

They stepped down from the space telescope's small transporter pad, and McCoy led her down the short corridor to the station's tiny control room. A small table and chairs had been set up there among the consoles, replete with candles and a bottle of champagne on ice. Nadja picked up one of the sporks set with the dinner plates and smiled, and McCoy knew his point total for the night was reaching high-score levels.

But the pièce de résistance was the station's main viewer, leaning out from the wall, just behind the table. There you could see whatever the telescope had been trained on, and just then it was pointed at a particularly stunning region of space, with towering greenish-brown gas clouds punctuated with glowing, pink, gemlike stars.

"Oh. I think I can see my house from here," Nadja said appreciatively.

"Not unless you live in the Eagle Nebula, you can't," McCoy told her. "They call that the Pillars of Creation. That column of gas coming off the nebula there is one hundred trillion kilometers high."

Nadja squeezed his arm close to her. "It's beautiful."

"It's a cautionary tale. That image you're seeing right there, that column of gas? It's long gone. Dead. Take a starship out there to see it, and you'll find out it's already been destroyed by a supernova shockwave. Light travels so slow, and it's so far away, the Argos telescope won't see it destroyed for another five hundred years."

Nadja tapped on his head. "Do you see doom and gloom in *everything* in space?"

"Just about," McCoy said. He put his arms around Nadja's waist. "But there's one thing in space right now that isn't so bad."

"Oh ho. Nice save," she told him. She gave him a kiss and then turned to the table. "So, what's for dinner?"

"Oh, garçon?" McCoy called.

There was a fumbling, crashing sound from the corridor that lead to the rest of the station, and McCoy rolled his eyes. Jim Kirk appeared in the doorway dressed in white tails and carrying a towel over his arm.

"Ah! *Bonjour*, madame and monsieur, and welcome to Chez Argos," he said. After McCoy had bailed out Jim from having to walk across campus all by his lonesome, he'd pressed Kirk into playing waiter for him. Nadja laughed again and took her seat after Kirk had pulled it out for her. He pulled out McCoy's chair next.

"Ixnay on the dead ars-stay," Kirk whispered in McCoy's ear as he sat. McCoy scowled and waved him away.

"Are you our waiter?" Nadja asked.

"Either that, or I'm a flag admiral," Kirk said. "I can't tell which."

"We'll start with the champagne," McCoy told him. If he let Kirk go on, Nadja would end up talking to Jim all night, not him.

"Ah. Chateau Picard," Kirk said, reading the label. "Never heard of it."

"Just pour already," McCoy ordered, exasperated.

Kirk popped the cork, and it caromed off into the consoles somewhere. Nadja smiled at McCoy across the table as Kirk poured their drinks. Under the table, her legs found his, and he nearly jumped.

McCoy cleared his throat. "Uh, thank you, garçon. I think we'll have the fish and then you can go. By which I mean am-scray."

CH.14.30
Dog Fight

Early the next morning, Kirk crossed the empty, secure campus alone, watching warily for Finnegan. He knew better than to call Bones in for escort duty again this time, not because it would anger his best friend, but because he had a feeling Bones wouldn't even answer his communicator. Bones hadn't come home last night after Kirk left him and Nadja together at "Chez Argos," which Kirk took to mean the night had been a success. He smiled at the thought of all the planning Bones had put into that one, and reminded himself to get Bones to help him the next time he had a big night to plan. Maybe Bones could help him put something special together for the Deltan cadet Areia. . . .

First up with Lartal this morning was another round with the linguistics team. Then more sessions at the medical conference. After Velocity yesterday, Lartal had spent the rest of the day attending seminars, grumbling the entire time about not being able to leave the campus. He hadn't taken notes like all the other doctors from the other planets, hadn't participated in any of the Q & A sessions, and once had even fallen asleep during a session. Kirk only knew because he himself had fallen asleep in the same seminar and then jerked awake, hurriedly glancing at Lartal to see if he'd noticed. Kirk was more and more convinced that Lartal was no doctor. But then why had he come?

Kirk checked in with the duty chief—not the chief who was out to get him, but some other chief he'd never met before—and went into the conference room, where two cadets stood pretending to be furniture, as he and Leslie had done.

"At ease, boys. It's too early," Kirk told them.

Unlike Leslie, they weren't friendly or chatty. Kirk didn't care. He welcomed the chance to close his eyes and get a little rest before he had to keep himself awake at medical seminars all day.

The outside door slid open, and a familiar voice said, "Shift change. I'll take over from here, boys."

Kirk opened his eyes. Finnegan stood in the doorway. The two cadets working the Added Security Detail in the corners smiled cruelly and walked out past Finnegan and into the hall, leaving Kirk and Finnegan alone.

"A little bird told me you come here every morning to

walk the dog, Jimmy boy," Finnegan said. "So I thought I'd stop chasing you and meet you somewhere you can't run. There's only two ways out of this room, Kirk. One of them goes to the dog pound. The other goes out into the hall, where my friends are gonna stand guard and make sure nobody disturbs us."

Finnegan cracked his knuckles and pulled a spork out of his pocket.

Kirk immediately assessed his options and stood. "You know what, Finnegan? I'm tired of running, anyway. So here's what I'm going to do. I'm going to beat you to a pulp *without* you touching me with that spork."

"I'd like to see you try it," Finnegan retorted.

Kirk grabbed the edge of the table, shoving it at Finnegan and ramming him in the stomach. Finnegan doubled over, and Kirk threw himself across the table, knocking the big cadet back into the wall. A flower vase on a pedestal rocked and fell, dumping its contents onto an imported Bajoran rug near the door. Finnegan got a good punch into Kirk's stomach, and Kirk rolled away. Finnegan stood again, spork in hand and murder on his face, and Kirk snatched up the end of the rug, yanking it out from under Finnegan's feet. He slammed into the ground with a thud, and Kirk hopped onto him, holding the rug between them so he couldn't be tapped with the spork. They pushed and shoved and punched through the rug until Finnegan finally got a knee up, and while it didn't catch Kirk where it would cause the most pain, it was painful enough. Finnegan shoved Kirk off and tossed the rug away, and Kirk took a step back to get out of spork range.

"You're gonna need that doctor roommate of yours when I get through with you, Jimmy boy," Finnegan told him.

"You're going to need every doctor at this medical conference to figure out what *species* you are when I'm through with *you*, Finnegan. Matter of fact, I wouldn't mind knowing that now."

Finnegan lunged for him, and Kirk threw a chair in his way to trip him up. They traded body blows, ducking and jabbing like prizefighters, both forgetting the Assassination Game and just fighting now out of pure hatred for each other.

The door to the Varkolak rooms slid open, and Lartal and his two Varkolak escorts came in.

"What's this?" Lartal said. The room was a disaster area, and Kirk and Finnegan didn't look much better.

Kirk used the surprise of Lartal's interruption to put a shoulder into Finnegan and send him to the floor again. While he was down, Kirk ran to the other side of the table, near Lartal.

"Looks like I'm safe," Kirk told Finnegan.

"They're not people, Kirk. They don't count," Finnegan

told him. He got up and brandished his spork again.

Lartal looked from Kirk to Finnegan and back again. He barked a command to his guards in Varkolak. Lartal grabbed Kirk and dragged him into the Varkolak common room behind them. Before Kirk could ask what he was doing, Lartal flipped open a large luggage crate and pushed him down inside it.

"Hide here," Lartal told him.

"Wait, no, I can take care of—" Kirk started to say, but Lartal pushed his head down and closed the lid. It was dark and tight inside, and there were still pieces of equipment in the bottom, stabbing into his butt and back. Worse, Kirk wasn't sure there were airholes. He pounded on the lid, calling for Lartal to let him out, but Lartal kicked the crate to silence him, and he heard Finnegan's voice.

"Where is he? I know he's still in here. Let me see what's in that crate."

Kirk heard Lartal growl menacingly, and shivered. Even here, in the relative safety of the crate, the sound made his skin crawl instinctively. It was an animal sound. Feral. The kind of sound that had sent Homo erectus running for their caves two million years ago. Finnegan was apparently still enough of a caveman to feel the flight instinct too, and Kirk heard the sound of the door whisking shut before Lartal unlatched the crate and let him out.

Kirk gasped for air and climbed out, clutching the back of a chair for support.

"It is a *ZanpantzarrRak*, isn't it?" Lartal asked excitedly.

"I don't know—I don't know what that means," Kirk said, still panting.

"You and the other. A chase. A game you are playing." Lartal's tail wagged quickly.

Kirk nodded. "Kind of."

Lartal frowned. "Is he your mate, then?"

"*What?* No," Kirk said. *What a weird question.*

The door to the conference room slid open, and Uhura stepped through.

"Kirk? What in the world is going on? The conference room looks like a tornado blew through." Behind her, Kirk and Lartal could see the linguistics team and the other two Varkolak surveying the damage.

"He has been playing at *ZanpantzarrRak*!" Lartal pushed past Uhura to speak animatedly in Varkolak to his companions in the other room. The linguists, excited to hear so much natural speech, quickly set to activating the big computer they brought with them as the door slid shut.

"Kirk? What's going on?"

"It's kind of a long story," Kirk told her. "And it's not a big deal. The Varkolak don't seem to care, anyway."

Kirk thought Uhura would read him the riot act, but she was staring instead into the open luggage crate. She glanced back at Kirk, reached in, and pulled out a Varkolak scanner. It must have been one of the things in the bottom of the crate poking him in the back.

Uhura slipped the scanner into her satchel and snapped it shut.

Kirk was incredulous. "Wait a minute, Uhura," he whispered. "You can't just—"

The door to the conference room opened again, and one of the linguistics officers stood in the doorway.

"Cadet Uhura, we're ready to begin. Is everything all right?"

"Yes," she said.

Kirk opened his mouth to say something, but Uhura cut him off with a pleading look. When the linguistics officer turned away, Kirk grabbed Uhura's arm and held her back. "Uhura, what do you think you're doing?"

"Later, Kirk," she whispered back. "I promise I'll explain everything. *Please*."

Kirk let her go and said nothing more about it, but this one was going to need some serious explaining. And soon.

CH.15.30
Cloak and Dagger

Kirk hurried around the side of the building to catch Uhura before she slipped away. He was doing a lot of running and chasing lately, he realized, only this time it was deadly serious.

He caught her jogging the back way toward the dorms and ran her down, grabbing her arm again to stop her.

"Hold up, Uhura. We have to talk."

"I said *later*, Kirk!" she whispered.

"It *is* later. Look, I didn't say a word back there the whole time you and everybody else were with Lartal, because I *know* you, Uhura. At least I thought I did. But I can't just let this go."

Uhura glanced around to see if anyone was watching them. There was a Starfleet Security officer heading across the quad toward the communications building, but she hadn't seen Uhura and Kirk yet. Uhura huffed and pulled Kirk behind a statue of Yuri Gagarin, where they wouldn't be seen. Kirk put a hand to her satchel to unlatch it, but she wouldn't let him.

"Don't."

"This is not cool, Uhura. What you did . . . It's not right. No matter why you did it. Do you really think stealing one of those things is going to make that much difference for Starfleet?"

"I didn't steal it to turn over to Starfleet. Not directly."

Kirk raised his palms as if to say, "Why, then?"

"I can't tell you. You're just going to have to trust me."

"I'm going to need a little more than that, Uhura. Starfleet doesn't just go around stealing from our guests, no matter how guilty we think they are. There's a high moral ground here, and the Federation owns a house with a view on it. You know what happens if it gets out you stole that thing? We're talking interplanetary *war* here!"

"I know! Don't you think I know that?" Uhura said. She sat down at the base of Yuri's statue, putting her head in her hands.

"Is someone—is someone making you do this?" Kirk asked.

"No." Uhura moaned. She looked up at Kirk, as if sizing him up, though he couldn't imagine what she was looking for in his face that she hadn't already seen there a hundred times before. She seemed to come to some sort of new decision about him.

"I'm working to help bring down a secret society at school."

"What?" Kirk sat down beside her.

Uhura told him all about it: a secret group called the Graviton Society, dedicated to protecting the Federation at all costs. How she was working at the request of someone higher up in Starfleet—she wouldn't say who—and how she was trying to gain more access to the organization by carrying out the first of their orders: steal a Varkolak "sniffer."

"Get you closer to who?" Kirk asked. "Who's behind it all?"

Uhura gave him one of her patented eye rolls. "If I knew that, it wouldn't be much of a secret society now, would it?"

It was all a bit much to believe, but then again, it was too crazy to be made up. And Kirk trusted Uhura. He might still be after her for her first name after all this time, but he counted her among his friends at the Academy. He *had* to believe her.

And then there was Bones and his Federation First medical cadet. Bones had just told him he suspected this Tellarite was up to no good, and now Uhura was telling him there was a whole group, a whole *society* of people, up to no good at the Academy. He felt his optimistic, naive view of Starfleet come crashing down, like a starship in the atmosphere. But if this medical cadet was involved, what would he want with a Varkolak sniffer?

"Do you know if this cadet, Daagen, is one of the Gravitons? He's a Tellarite."

Uhura shook her head. "I've never seen any of them without cloaks on. I just don't know."

Kirk stood. "I want to help. Get me an invite. I'll go undercover with you."

Uhura laughed. "Ah, no."

"What? Why?"

"You? Kirk, they'd see you coming a mile away. Subtlety is not your strong suit."

"No?" Kirk smirked. "So what *is* my strong suit?"

"Your overweening arrogance."

Kirk pointed a finger at her. "That's *something* you like. That's one thing."

Uhura stood. "Please, Kirk. Just . . . don't rat me out. I promise it's for the right reasons."

"All right," Kirk told her. "But I hate this cloak-and-dagger nonsense."

Uhura sighed. "Me too."

Leonard McCoy hated all this cloak-and-dagger nonsense.

He'd kept an eye on Daagen all afternoon in the lab, trying to catch him doing something suspicious, and when he'd failed to do that, he'd followed him—surreptitiously, he hoped—across campus to his dorm. Now he sat on a bench across the courtyard, pretending to read something on his PADD while really watching the door for Daagen to reemerge.

Maybe Jim was right, after all. Maybe it was crazy to think anyone who would willingly enroll in Starfleet would ever do something illicit, even if they thought it was for the greater good. Starfleet was about *ideals*, damn it. It was about seeking out new life and new civilizations, boldly going where no one had gone before. Not to conquer the galaxy, but to explore it. To learn from it.

"Oh, this is just ridiculous," he told two pigeons strutting nearby.

McCoy cycled down his PADD and stuffed it back into his satchel. He was ready to go get something to eat in the cafeteria and forget all this stupidity when Daagen emerged from his dorm carrying a knapsack. The Tellarite looked around furtively, then headed off at a quick pace. Away from the main campus.

McCoy cursed himself inwardly, but he followed, anyway.

"Leonard!" someone called. It was Nadja. She was waving to him from across the quad. If she called out again, Daagen might hear her and turn around. McCoy hurried to intercept her, signaling to her to be quiet, and pulled her along behind a statue of Yuri Gagarin.

"Whoa, reduce to impulse engines, Leonard," she said with a laugh.

McCoy peeked out from behind the statue. Daagen was just turning the corner of the barracks where the Varkolak were stationed. *The Varkolak!*

"Come on," McCoy told Nadja. "But be quiet."

"Are we hunting wabbits?" she asked as they skulked along.

"No. Spies. Maybe. I don't know. You know Daagen, that fellow I was telling you about? The one who gave me back your communicator? I've been watching him. He just left his dorm with a knapsack."

"Oh no. Do you think . . . do you think he plans on doing some *knapping*? Or"—she gasped exaggeratedly— "dare I say it, some *sacking*?"

"Laugh all you want, but he's up to something. I know it."

But whatever he was up to, it didn't have anything to do with the Varkolak. Daagen left campus, and soon after, ducked into a public restroom. Nadja and McCoy hid in a shop across the street, watching through the front display window.

"You wait here," Nadja whispered. "I'll go in and see if he's executing secret plan number one or secret plan number two."

"Cut it out," McCoy said.

"Look, he couldn't have anything too incriminating in that knapsack. He had to get past the security guards in the dorm just to leave with it."

"If you want to go back, go back," McCoy told her.

A cloaked figure emerged from the bathrooms, looked around, and continued down the road, away from campus. On campus, something like that would have stood out among all the redshirted cadets and their blue-uniformed instructors. On the streets around San Francisco, an intergalactic port of call, no one would bat an eye.

"Okay, *that's* suspicious," Nadja said.

"Do you think that was him?" McCoy asked.

"He was the same height," she said. "And he was carrying the same knapsack."

"Well? What did I tell you?" McCoy asked.

"Lead on, secret agent man. Lead on."

Hikaru Sulu tugged at the oversized sleeves of his robe, feeling stupid. Why had he agreed to do this again? He sighed. He hated all this cloak-and-dagger nonsense, but at least the hood kept the others from knowing who he was. Then again, he didn't know who they were, either. He looked around at the other nine hooded and robed people waiting with him in the dingy back room of a Sausalito dive bar. Who were these people? Did he know any of them? Were they in his classes with him? Did one of them sit next to him in exobotany? The only Graviton he knew was his contact, Daagen, a medical cadet, which was exactly how the Graviton Society wanted it.

"We're all here," one of the hooded figures said. "Let's do this. Report."

"Our plan to explose the mole failed," one of them said. From his voice, Sulu recognized him as Daagen.

"Was the information given to the suspect?"

Everyone was quiet, and Sulu realized they were expecting him to speak. It had been his job, after all. "Oh. Um, yes. I did. I told her. Everything, just as we discussed. She bit—hook, line, and sinker."

"I can verify that contact was made," said another voice; a woman. "I was in the gym that morning. I saw him engage her."

Sulu blanched underneath his hood. Someone had been there? Watching him? Making sure he did his job? He shook it off. He should have known better. Should have realized they would do that. He was a newbie, after all. He had to prove they could trust him.

"Perhaps we were wrong. Perhaps she's not connected to the mole."

"Perhaps he's not a mole, after all," said another.

"I still say he can't be trusted. He's Vulcan."

"Vulcans can be devilish creatures," said another cool voice. "Let us not forget the P'Jem incident."

"That was a hundred years ago! Let it go, already!"

"I'm just saying," said the cool voice that Sulu now figured was Andorian. "They have been known to be devious."

"It's not that he's a Vulcan that worries me," said another woman. "It's that he is the ultimate company man. He has to be a plant."

"He's certainly as stiff as one," someone joked.

"Enough," said the voice that had begun the proceedings. "We will have to approach the target directly. The floor is open to—"

The wooden door to the room flew open, and a red-faced cadet with fire in his eyes came rushing in.

"What do you think you're doing, sneaking around in robes and hiding out in smoky backrooms?" the man demanded. "Damn it, man, you're Starfleet cadets, not Romulan spies!"

Stunned by the sudden explosion, Sulu took a step back. It drew the angry cadet's attention, and he tried to whip off Sulu's hood. Sulu reacted instinctively. He grabbed the cadet's hand, delivered a quick but powerful chop to his stomach, then flipped him to the ground. Sulu recoiled in horror from his own actions, immediately sorry he'd hurt a fellow cadet. He looked around for some way out, wondering why the others were just standing there, when he felt the familiar tug of a transporter beam catching him up and scattering his atoms. . . .

Sulu rematerialized on a transporter pad he didn't recognize. There were two other Gravitons with him on the pad, but no transporter operator. The room was empty but for the transporter's three passengers.

The other two stepped down off the pad and hurried for the door.

"Wait!" Sulu called.

One of them hung back while the other ran.

"What's happened? Where are we?" Sulu asked.

"You must be the new guy," said the Graviton. It wasn't Daagen's voice, nor anyone else's he recognized. "By the looks of it, we're in the engineering building, back on campus. We've always got people waiting to beam us out if we need an emergency evac. The others will have beamed back to other places. You're safe now. Just get someplace where you can lose the robe and then head back to your dorm or wherever. I don't know who that guy was, or how he found us, but those were some nice moves you put on him. Shields up," he said, and hurried from the room.

"Yeah, shields up," Sulu said, beginning to understand that the Graviton Society was a lot bigger and a lot better organized than he had ever imagined.

• · · ⁺ ⁚ ✦ • ✦ ·· ·

Nadja helped McCoy up from the sticky floor of the dive bar's backroom and brushed him off.

"Son of a bitch," McCoy said.

"Are you badly hurt?"

"No. It's not that," he said, rubbing his stomach. Probably a hematoma of the rectus abdominis muscle, he quickly diagnosed, then reminded himself there were more pressing issues. "They transported out, the cowards. Transported out! Secret societies and their damned secret clubhouse meetings, working against everything we swore an oath to uphold—"

Nadja pulled him into a hard, passionate kiss, and his anger about the group's escape evaporated. When she finally let him go, he felt like he'd been caught up in a transporter beam himself and deposited in someplace entirely new, where the gravity was half that of Earth normal.

"What was that for?" he asked.

"You," she said, not letting him go. "Charging in here, like Archer against the Xindi. You're my hero."

She kissed him again, and he was transported somewhere there was no gravity at all.

"Come on. Let's get out of here," she told him.

"Shouldn't we wait for the police?"

"And show them what? An empty room? I can think of better ways to spend the night. I just want to do one thing first," Nadja said.

"What's that?"

"Stop by my room and get my toothbrush," she told him with a smile.

CH.16.30
A Game of Chase

James T. Kirk could barely keep his eyes open.

It wasn't just that he'd slept in the library all night long while Bones was entertaining a guest (Bones had certainly returned the favor plenty enough times that Kirk wasn't put out about it). It was the medical lectures. It was bad enough he zoned out when Bones started talking medicine, but to hear these doctors get going, you'd think Bones was just a kid with one of those games that buzzed when you tried to take out the funny bone. These were some seriously heavy hitters in the interplanetary constellation of medicine, with enough data to choke a sehlat.

Or put a layman like Kirk to sleep.

Lartal wasn't faring much better, although today he wasn't dozing off. Today he was restless. He tapped his paws on the table in front of him so much the J'naii doctor beside him had to shush him, and his wagging tail thumped against the table behind him.

Clapping snapped Kirk awake, and he realized the session was over.

"Let's go, Kirk. I need to move," Lartal told him.

Kirk couldn't agree more. At least they would have fifteen or twenty minutes to stretch their legs before the next session began. Lartal was immediately flanked by his equally bored Varkolak escorts and then by the four just-as-bored Starfleet Security officers assigned to him for the morning. Kirk couldn't feel too sorry for them—at least they got a shift change at lunchtime.

Lartal's complicated entourage made its way from the great hall slowly, just like everyone else, as two thousand nattering doctors clogged the few exits out to the lobby and the old parade grounds beyond.

"Rather be playing chase, wouldn't you, Kirk?" Lartal asked.

"Anything," Kirk said. "Anything besides this. But of course, as a doctor, you find this all terribly fascinating, I'm sure."

"Terribly," Lartal growled.

Finally, they got past the doors and into the lobby, which was loud with the echoed conversations of all the doctors. A refreshment table was set up along one side, and multiple bathroom facilities along the other wall were already drawing lines. Kirk figured Lartal would go for one or the other, but he suddenly found himself cut off from Lartal by his two big Varkolak companions.

"Hey, guys, coming through," Kirk said. He tried to squeeze between them, but they closed ranks even farther, keeping him from getting through.

Kirk had a very bad feeling about this.

He turned to Johnson, one of the two security officers behind them. "Do you have Lartal? Where is he?"

"We've got him," Johnson said confidently. He flipped open his communicator. "Forlax, you've got Lartal up there with you, right?"

"What?" came the voice of Forlax over Johnson's communicator. "No. We thought he was back there with you."

Johnson's eyes went wide, and Kirk knew they were all in big, big trouble. He barreled through the two Varkolak, but Lartal wasn't there. He jumped, trying to see over the mass of people in the room, but Lartal was nowhere to be seen.

The two Varkolak guards snickered.

"Stay with them!" Johnson ordered his partner and Kirk, and he moved off calling for the building to be sealed off. Kirk saw more security officers converging on the front doors, but Lartal was smart. He had to know they'd lock him in the moment they lost him, and he'd never try something so obvious as to storm the front doors. That meant he had to find some other way out . . .

The stairs. Kirk thought it before he saw it, hidden away behind the lines of people queueing for the bathrooms.

Ignoring the indignant cries of the people he pushed out of the way, Kirk swam through the ocean of doctors and researchers toward the far wall.

"Sorry, people! Coming through! Bathroom emergency!" he said. That made more people get out of his way, but it was still agonizingly slow going. He finally got to the door to the stairs and pushed his way inside. The door slid closed with a quiet *whomph* and *click*, and suddenly the cacophany of the lobby was all but gone.

And replaced by faint sound of padded feet running up stairs.

"Lartal!" Kirk called. "Lartal, don't do this!"

A high-pitched, playful sound echoed down the stairwell—somewhere between a laugh and a bark—and Kirk cursed inwardly.

Here we go again, he thought, and he took off at a run.

Eight floors up, Kirk heard one of the stairwell's exterior doors hissing shut, and he plowed through it. On the far side of the roof, Lartal was just dropping down over the side.

"Damn it!" Kirk said as he ran. "I knew a tour of the building was a bad idea."

The assembly hall was enormous, built like a series of toy blocks stacked up in a sort of ziggurat shape. Lartal had led him straight up to the top of the stairs, and now he was going to go all the way back down, from rooftop to rooftop.

"I thought dogs didn't like to climb," Kirk complained.

He slid to a stop at the edge of the roof, looking down. Lartal's grinning jackal face glanced up at Kirk before he leaped onto the next rooftop below, and ran for the corner of the building.

"Lartal! This isn't funny! If you want to play chase, we can do it in the sports complex!"

Lartal wasn't listening. He ran with all the pent-up energy of someone forced to sit and listen to xenobiology lectures all day. But so did Kirk. As much as he hated to admit it, he felt alive again, in his element once more. Give him action. Give him adventure. Give him danger.

He slid down the ladder to gain ground on Lartal and hit the surface too fast, landing on the gravel rooftop elbows first.

I hope he gets a scratched-up right elbow, he thought. No time to cry over it, though. He put his hand to it, to staunch the bleeding as he ran, but he eventually abandoned it altogether. He didn't have time to be hurt. Lartal was already heading down the next ladder.

Kirk followed him as fast as he could, taking this stretch more slowly, so as not to have a repeat of his fall. He saw Lartal run off toward the east side of the building, and he smiled. If he was right, the next ladder down was on the *west* side of the building, not the east. It was one of the ones you could see from the old parade grounds out front. He hit the rooftop and ran the opposite direction.

"Gotcha!" Kirk cried as he rounded the corner, but he pulled up short. The ladder was there, but Lartal wasn't. Kirk ran to the edge of the rooftop to look down. Lartal *couldn't* have beaten him around two sides of the building in the time it took Kirk to turn the corner. And he hadn't. Lartal wasn't on the ladder, either. Had he doubled back and gone up again? But what for? Was this just a game for him, a chase to work off his restlessness or—

"No. Damn it!" Kirk cried. Of course. He'd been so stupid. He sprinted around to the north side of the building in time to see Lartal scrambling up the side of Surak Hall, the closest building to the assembly hall. Kirk gauged the distance between the two rooftops for a jump, but his brain immediately told him it was impossible. For a human. But apparently not for a Varkolak. Or a Varkolak trained in athletics, like Lartal.

"There's no way you're a doctor!" Kirk called across the chasm.

Lartal smiled and saluted Kirk, as if to acknowledge it. "I'm sorry, Kirk! I just want you to know that—"

But Kirk never heard the rest because the building beneath him exploded, and he fell.

CH.17.30
Usual and Unusual Suspects

The Academy hospital was chaos again. Doctors were tripping over themselves to see to the victims of this second—and more deadly—bomb blast. Most of the victims were doctors themselves, and wanted a hand in deciding their own treatments, which only complicated matters. Still, it could have been worse: The bomb had exploded inside the great hall during a session break, sparing everyone in the lobby from the blast. But forty-six people were wounded and thirteen were dead—including, word had it, Admiral Wójcik, the head of Starfleet Medical.

McCoy hurried from biobed to biobed, treating cuts and breaks and bruises. As he worked, he felt like he'd been here before, already had this nightmare, but he worked on without comment. This was no time to lose his head.

A new patient was brought in, later than all the others,

and McCoy hurried over when he recognized the familiar face.

"Jim! Jim, what's happened?" McCoy asked, but his friend didn't answer. Kirk's eyes were closed, and he had swelling on his face. One of his pant legs was torn and bloody.

"One of the Varkolak just brought him in," a nurse told him. "Looks like a broken fibula, multiple scrapes and bruises, and he's got second-degree burns on his back and posterior."

McCoy ran his medical tricorder over Jim and checked the biobed readings to confirm the diagnosis. "He's also got some internal bleeding," he said. "Get me ten ccs of hydrocortilene and prepare another hypospray with kelotane for the burns. We need to get him stabilized."

McCoy put a cortical stimulator on Kirk's forehead and activated it, syncing it with the biobed. The nurse handed him the hydrocortilene hypospray, and he double-checked it before injecting it into Kirk's neck. "Cut that uniform away. And get me an osteoregenerator," McCoy called, although the nurse was probably already on it.

"Bones." Kirk moaned.

"I'm here, Jim. You're going to be all right. By tomorrow you'll be back to chasing skirts."

"The Varkolak . . ." Jim muttered.

"The Varkolak set the bomb," someone said from the

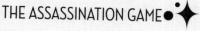

next biobed over. It was Daagen, tending to a patient there. "It's clear now. They should be expelled. It may even mean war."

"No," Kirk muttered.

McCoy's blood began to boil. "Last time I checked, in the Federation, people were innocent until proven guilty, Daagen."

"How many people have to die before you and the rest of the idealistic fools in Starfleet come to your senses?" Daagen argued.

Kirk grabbed McCoy's tunic and pulled him close. "Lartal . . . He ran away. I chased him. Up on the roof . . ."

"Yes, apparently he's the one who brought you in. Now, hush. I'm just going to re-set this bone. You won't feel a thing."

McCoy prepped a hypospray with fifteen ccs of anetrizine and injected it into Kirk's leg. The nurse handed him the osteoregenerator and he tweaked the intensity. "Have a tri-laser connector and a dermal regenerator standing by," he told his nurse. When he glanced up, he saw two security officers headed his way.

"You there," he told them. "Keep an eye on that man." He pointed at Daagen. "That man's a menace."

Daagen sneered at him from across his patient's biobed, but the security officers didn't seem to be interested. They flanked McCoy instead.

"Cadet Leonard McCoy?" one of them asked. "I'm afraid you're going to have to come with us."

"I can't answer questions right now, damn it. Can't you see I'm about to perform surgery?"

"I'm afraid you're under arrest, sir."

"Arrest? What in the Sam Hill are you talking about, man? For what?"

"For possible involvement in the shuttle explosion."

McCoy couldn't believe what he was hearing. "Is this—is this a joke? It's damn poor timing, if it is."

"I'm afraid it's no joke, sir. If you'll put down the instrument and please come with us."

The doctors and nurses at the surrounding beds stared at him, and McCoy felt his already barely organized world spinning out of control. The next biobed over, Daagen smirked at his misfortune. *Daagen*. If the Tellarite was behind this . . .

One of the security officers put a hand to McCoy's arm, and he jerked away involuntarily.

"No," Jim whispered from the biobed. "No, officers, he couldn't have—" he tried to say, but that was all he had. He needed surgery, and he needed it *now*.

The security officer took his arm again, and this time McCoy couldn't shake him off.

"There is a medical crisis going on!" Bones protested as they pulled the osteoregenerator from his hand and dragged him toward the door. "I'm a qualified physician being taken away in the middle of a medical procedure! This is preposterous!"

"Don't worry," Daagen called. He stood beside Kirk's bed now, osteoregenerator in hand. "I'll take care of your friend."

• · . ✦ ·· ✦ · ✦ ·· .

Admiral Barnett set a scarred, twisted piece of metal on the table with a thunk.

"Is this supposed to impress me in some way?" Lartal asked. He and the rest of the Varkolak contingent—doctors, security, and staff—sat in chairs on the other side of the table, surrounded by a small army of Starfleet Security officers.

"It's certainly made an impression on us," Barnett said. "This is one of your sniffer devices. Or what's left of it. Our investigators found it in the wreckage of this morning's explosion in the assembly hall. It was used to trigger the explosive device that killed thirteen people and injured forty-seven more."

"I don't recognize it," Lartal said.

At the far end of the table, Uhura felt the world drop out from under her. *She* recognized it. It was the sniffer she had stolen from the Varkolak's compound. The scanning device she had passed on to her contact in the Graviton

Society, under Spock's direction. Thirteen people killed. Forty-seven injured. And *she* had been the one to give the bomber the detonation device.

"Do you deny this is one of your scanners?"

The Varkolak picked it up, sniffed at it, then put it back on the table. "No. But we had a similar device stolen from our quarters just the other day."

"Stolen," the admiral said, his voice dripping with sarcasm. "Right. And I don't suppose you reported this alleged theft."

Lartal sat back in his chair. "Why should we report a theft to the very people who stole it?"

"You think Starfleet stole your scanner," Barnett said.

"Starfleet, or someone acting on its behalf. Who else would do it? Who else had access? We are being framed for this tragedy, Admiral. Or perhaps you know that already."

Only Lartal was defiant. The rest of the Varkolak looked cowed, their ears downturned. Uhura couldn't help but feel the same way. If she had a tail, it would most certainly be between her legs. Lartal was right. She was the thief. Someone *was* framing them for this. She knew she should say something, but she was afraid. It wasn't just her Starfleet career. That was finished. It was the scandal it would cause. The fallout it would bring. Maybe even a war.

She had to talk to Spock. He would know how best to handle it. They would have to come clean, about everything, but he would know how best to do it.

The door to the interrogation room slid open, and Kirk hobbled through. He looked like hell. His face was bruised, his chest was bandaged, and he was favoring his right leg. Uhura's heart sank. Kirk knew she had taken the sniffer. The truth would most certainly come out now, before she could figure out a way to soften the blow.

"Admiral, sir. I'm sorry I'm late," Kirk said. "The doctors weren't too keen on letting me out of sickbay."

"Go back, Kirk. We don't need you here right now," Barnett told him.

"Are you accusing Lartal of setting that bomb in the assembly hall?"

"I said *go back*, Kirk. That's an order."

Lartal stood. "Wait. I am being accused of a crime, am I not? Under your law, I believe I am afforded the right to an advocate, yes?"

The admiral frowned. "Yes, but—"

"I choose Kirk as my advocate, if he will agree."

Kirk studied the Varkolak for a moment, then nodded. "But we're going to need some answers, Lartal. All of us."

Lartal didn't say no.

"You came back for me, didn't you? After the explosion," Kirk said. "They told me you were the one who brought me to the hospital."

"I did."

"And that's where you were apprehended, wasn't it?"

"It was," Lartal growled.

"But there is the sniffer, Kirk," Admiral Barnett said. "One of their scanners was used to detonate the bomb."

"Which was *stolen* from us," Lartal reiterated.

"A sniffer was used to—" Kirk said, putting it all together. Kirk turned to look at Uhura, but she kept her head down. He had every excuse to expose her now, every right. She decided she wouldn't deny it, and she braced herself for the revelation.

"You . . . have to admit it's possible, Admiral," Kirk said. "There are a dozen people in and out of the Varkolak rooms every day."

Uhura looked up, on the brink of tears. He hadn't called her out. Hadn't told them what he knew. He spared her an anguished glance, but that was all.

"Are you suggesting someone from Starfleet would actually steal one of their devices, Kirk? And what, blow up their own assembly hall, kill their own people, just to implicate the Varkolak? I refuse to believe it."

"I agree. But why would Lartal walk right back into the hands of Starfleet to bring me to the hospital if he was the one who set the bomb? Why would he care if I bled to death on that rooftop or not? He had gotten away from me and the security detail. I'd lost him. He was free."

"And what was he doing, running from you and the

security detail in the first place?" the admiral asked.

For that, Kirk had no answer. He turned to Lartal. "It's now or never, Lartal. Are you going to tell us why you're really here? I know you're not a doctor."

"It is time to tell the truth!" one of the Varkolak doctors exclaimed.

Lartal twisted in his chair and growled, then barked something in Varkolak. "'I will determine . . . decide something to say,'" Uhura translated without thinking. "Maybe 'I will decide what to say.'" The Varkolak doctor put her head down quickly and was silent.

"Lartal, she's right," Kirk told him. "If there's a reason that could help, you need to tell us."

Lartal growled, then seemed to relent.

"ZanpantzarrRak," he said.

Kirk frowned. "That word. You used it before. When Finnegan was after me."

"'The chase,'" Uhura said, despite herself. "'The pursuit.'"

Kirk put it together. "You're chasing someone. That's why you wanted to get off campus. Why you scanned everything, why you marked where you'd been. You're chasing someone who's in San Francisco."

"Chasing someone? Here on Earth?" Admiral Barnett said. "Who?"

Lartal looked away.

"His mate," Kirk said, and Uhura and everyone else in

the room looked at him in surprise. "That's what you meant when you asked me if Finnegan was my mate, didn't you? I didn't understand what you were talking about."

Lartal nodded reluctantly. "The *ZanpantzarrRak* is an age-old ritual on my planet. An institution. When we mate, the female runs someplace far away and difficult to track, forcing the male to find her. In the past, it was a test of his tracking abilities, allowing only the best and strongest males to mate. A means of selective breeding, as I'm sure the doctors can elaborate. Today it is a ritual we honor to keep our hearts and minds wild."

"You're telling me there's a Varkolak *here*, on Earth, hiding out in *San Francisco*? Impossible!" Admiral Barnett exclaimed.

Lartal smacked the table with his paw, making everyone jump. "Not impossible! Not for a woman like Gren! She is as clever as she is beautiful. To hide here, among our enemies, in this most difficult place to find her? It only proves her cunning."

Two or three of the other Varkolak males growled their approval, which didn't seem to offend Lartal in the least.

"'The doctors can elaborate,'" Kirk repeated. "That's what you said. Your mate, the chase—that's the only reason you're here, isn't it? You're not a doctor, are you?"

"No," he said. "I am a captain in the Varkolak Armada."

His words caused a stir in both camps. The Varkolak

had obviously known, and now despaired of the truth coming out. On the Starfleet side, the news made the storm clouds gathering around Admiral Barnett even darker.

"So. You admit you're here under false pretenses and you're a military officer, not a doctor," Admiral Barnett said. "And we're supposed to believe all this chase business?"

"For what it's worth, Admiral, I believe him," Kirk said.

Lartal nodded respectfully to Kirk, but Kirk's words didn't seem to hold much sway with the admiral.

"Do you have any proof, Kirk? For any of this?" Barnett asked.

Uhura felt Kirk's eyes on her again, and she stared at her hands.

"No, sir," Kirk said.

"Then your opinion is noted, as is *Captain* Lartal's testimony. The Varkolak will be detained in the Academy brig until further notice."

Lartal jumped to his feet. "This is an outrage! We have done nothing wrong!"

The security officers in the room converged on the Varkolak, phasers out and at the ready. Lartal's guards growled, but he silenced them.

"This will be seen as an act of war, Barnett," Lartal told him.

Admiral Barnett said nothing more as the security

officers led the Varkolak from the room. Uhura saw Kirk staring meaningfully at her again. She knew she had to come forward. She knew she had to say something. She just needed to talk to Spock first. Spock would know what to do.

She tried to say all that and more with her eyes, but she knew her desperate apology was no substitute for the truth. It would have to do, though, and she hurried from the room before Kirk asked her to say more.

Kirk watched Uhura go. If she kept her tongue, Lartal would hang for a crime he didn't commit, and two civilizations would go to war. He had to trust her to know what she was doing, but it couldn't wait long.

Admiral Barnett got up to leave, and Kirk caught him.

"Admiral, wait. Bones—Cadet McCoy—why was he arrested?"

"I'm sorry. I can't discuss it," Barnett told him.

"But what's he done? What's he been accused of?"

"Maybe starting a war, Kirk. If we didn't do that here just now already."

"Bones? Start a war? You can't be serious! What, you think he had something to do with the explosion today? Then why are you holding Lartal?"

The admiral sighed. When the last of the linguistics

team and security officers had left the room, he said quietly, "There is a possibility that the two incidents were initiated by different provocateurs."

"Different—But you can't be serious. Bones, bomb a shuttle? For what? How? Why?"

Barnett put up a hand. "I've said too much already. But they'll all remain in custody until this mess is settled. If it ever is. Go back to the hospital, Kirk. You look like hell."

"Aye, sir," Kirk said as the admiral left, but he had no intention of going back to the hospital. There were too many people he needed to talk to first.

CH.18.30
Suitable for Framing

This time Uhura wanted to see Spock. *Needed* to see him. But all thought of romance was gone from her mind. They were in *trouble*. That was all that mattered now. They were in trouble, and she needed him to fix it.

Spock was waiting for her in the observation deck.

"Cadet Uhura," he said as she hurried to him from the turbolift. "We must be careful. We are under suspicion by the Graviton Society. They have been feeding us false information."

"Spock—Spock, be quiet and listen to me. It's worse than that. Much worse than that. The sniffer. The Varkolak scanning device *I* stole. It was used to detonate that bomb."

Spock frowned. "I had not heard this."

"It hasn't been released yet. But I was there, Spock. I saw it with my own eyes. It was the scanner I took. The scanner I gave to the Graviton Society!" She told him all about the interrogation, including how she'd kept quiet about her involvement. "We're being *used*, Spock. *I've* been used. It's my fault all those people died!"

Spock put a hand on her shoulder. "Nyota. Be calm. It is not your fault people have died. It is the fault of whomever planted that bomb. No doubt they would have done so, whether or not we gave them the means to assign blame to the Varkolak or not. And yet . . . I am confused."

"About what?"

"Immediately following the incident in the assembly hall today, I was contacted by my source within the Graviton Society, with word that they mean to falsely implicate the Varkolak . . . after the fact."

Uhura huffed. "Spock, that's what I've been trying to tell you! They already have!"

"And therein lies my confusion," Spock explained. "Why would the Graviton Society feel the need to falsely implicate the Varkolak in the bombing if they had already done so with the detonation device?"

At last, Uhura thought she understood. She'd seen evidence of someone trying to pin the explosion on the Varkolak, evidence not everyone knew about, and now the Graviton Society was telling Spock they wanted to try and implicate the Varkolak in some other way. But why bother if they had already set them up by using the sniffer?

"Are you saying the Graviton Society didn't know the

sniffer was being used as the detonation device? That they *didn't* set the bomb?"

Spock walked away from her, holding his hands behind his back the way he did when he was thinking hard about something.

"The scanning device was given to someone within the Society," Spock said. "And yet those at the top of the organization do not know it was used in the explosion. Therefore, we must assume that someone along the line intercepted the Varkolak scanner and created a bomb with it, unknown to those in the chain above him or her."

"A rogue agent *within* the Graviton Society?" It was almost too dizzying a prospect. Wasn't all this confusing enough without someone within the secret society doing something even *more* secret? "But who? And why?"

"I do not have enough facts to draw a hypothesis, but we may assume, I think, that it is someone who regards the Graviton Society as not going far enough toward its goal."

That was a scary idea.

"For all we know, the Varkolak scanning device may never even have passed beyond your contact. You have no clue as to his or her identity?" Spock asked.

"No, although I'd wager it's a her. Otherwise he would have had some serious explaining to do if he'd been caught in the women's shower room."

"Indeed," Spock said.

"Wait, you said someone's been feeding us false information," Uhura said. "Are you sure this isn't more of the same?"

"Yes. This information was not passed on to me through the usual channels. It was relayed to me by . . . a trusted source within the group."

So Spock had more spies besides Uhura working for him. She'd been stupid to think he'd brought her in on this for any other reason than that the assignment required it. She felt herself getting upset again, and she put the emotion away. She still had bigger problems to deal with.

"Spock, we have to tell the truth. I have to tell them I took that sniffer. If I don't, it could mean war."

"It could mean war if you do," Spock told her. "While Starfleet will understand when Captain Pike and I explain my mission and your involvement in it, the Varkolak will believe what they will. Or won't, as the case may be."

"So what do we do, Spock? I can't just sit on this! I have a duty, damn it! I swore an oath to uphold the laws and traditions of Starfleet. We both did. And this is breaking about twenty of them."

"We will tell the truth," Spock assured her. "Together." He paused, thinking. "But not yet."

He was cooking up something. Uhura could see it in his eyes, the way they were staring off into the distance without really looking at anything. She waited for him to put it all together.

"This situation, and our particular knowledge of it, has presented us with a unique opportunity. We two are the only people within the Graviton Society who know that one of its members has gone rogue, and thus, the only two people who can exploit the situation to reveal the culprit."

"Exploit it? How?" Uhura asked.

"By running, as it is called on Earth, a 'con.'"

The security officers in the Academy brig scanned Kirk and let him through to see Bones, who came right up to the edge of the force field to see him.

"Jim! Jim, I've been framed. There's a secret society on campus, and they— What are you doing out of the hospital? Who signed your release? Daagen? He's part of all this!"

"Whoa, whoa, Bones. It's going to be all right. We'll get to the bottom of all this," Kirk told him, but he knew if their situations were reversed, he'd be just as frantic. Behind them, the security officers cleared another visitor, and Bones's new main squeeze, Nadja Luther, joined them.

"Leonard! I just heard! What in the world is going on?" she said.

"I've been framed, damn it!"

"Slow down and start from the beginning," Kirk told him.

"Somebody tampered with the evidence from the

shuttle bombing," Bones explained. "I know this, of course, because I've just been through four hours of *the same damn questions over and over again*. The night after the bombing, somebody went back into the lab using *my* voice-print identification and contaminated the debris with kemocite."

"The fuel the Varkolak use in their gadgets," Kirk said.

"It wasn't me, of course, but three people saw me leave the dorm that night on that snipe hunt to meet Nadja at Cavallo Point."

"And nobody saw you there," Nadja guessed.

"Of course not! It was the middle of the damn night. So naturally I have an alibi that's as full of holes as a Bolian sponge worm. And then, of course, it's me who discovers the kemocite in the lab the next morning, like I wanted to make sure everybody found it, when I was only running it through the phoretic analyzer. I was showing initiative, damn it!"

Kirk put up a hand to calm his friend. "Let's go back to the phone call from Nadja. The one that got you out of the way so someone could do all this and you wouldn't have an alibi for it."

"Not Nadja," she said. "It wasn't me."

"No. It was Daagen, that Federation First bastard. I'm sure of it. Next morning, he comes to me, smug as a Tarkanian pig, and tells me he just happened to find it on his desk."

"Did you tell Starfleet Security all of this?" Kirk asked.

"Of course I told them! But they already had their minds made up. They think I stole Nadja's communicator and called myself with it to give myself an alibi, then left it on Daagen's desk that night when I broke into the lab to slather kemocite all over everything."

"I don't understand," Nadja said. "What made them start looking into all this in the first place? Why assume the kemocite had been planted?"

"Apparently kemocite and plasma don't just go boom. They create a chain reaction until one of them is all used up. But there was kemocite *and* plasma on the wreckage. There shouldn't have been both."

"Unless someone planted it there, after the fact," Nadja finished for him.

"When they figured out that little puzzle, they went back to check the access records, and here I am. But wait. That's not the kicker. Jim, they found kemocite in our room."

"They *what*?"

"A canister of it. From the engineering building stores. In the closet behind that case of Saurian brandy I'm also not supposed to have." Bones raised his hands in surrender and paced his small cell.

"Somebody's working awfully hard to see you take the fall for this one, Bones," Kirk told him.

"It's that Tellarite, Daagen. I'm sure of it. Nadja and I followed him and his buddies to some kind of secret meeting down in Sausalito, but they beamed out before we could nab one of them. He's up to something, Jim. I told Starfleet Security all about that too, but they didn't believe it either, the buffoons!" Bones said, raising his voice so the guards at the brig door could hear him.

"I'll get to the bottom of it all, Bones," Kirk told him. "I promise."

"So do I," Nadja said.

"We should have plenty of time, too," Kirk said. "The Academy has canceled classes and suspended the end of semester exams until all this blows over."

"If it does," Nadja said. "Everybody's buzzing there might be a war with the Varkolak."

"Good god," Bones said.

"Yeah, you hope. But don't worry. I'll get you out of here, buddy," Kirk told him. The wheels were already turning. "And the first thing I'm going to need is your communicator."

Kirk got a few more answers out of Bones before leaving, and promised to meet up with Nadja later to let her know what he'd learned. On the way out of the brig, he was called over to another cell, where Lartal stood by the force field, as frantic and impatient as Bones had been.

"Kirk," Lartal said. "I wanted to thank you. For the way you stood up for me."

"I owed you one. Two, maybe," Kirk said. Lartal was still coy about whether or not he'd saved Kirk from the shuttle blast, but Kirk was pretty sure the Varkolak had saved his life twice.

"You are a man of honor," Lartal said. "Thank you."

Kirk nodded and left, feeling certain that two people in that brig were there under false arrest. He was determined to clear them both.

CH.19.30
The Fate of the Galaxy and All That

"Earlier today, the Varkolak Assembly denounced the arrests, calling for the immediate release of Captain Lartal and the other members of the Varkolak contingent here on Earth, but Federation officials assert that the Varkolak will not be released, pending the outcome of their investigation into the recent bombings. At this hour, FNS has reports that Starfleet is recalling its main fleet to Sector zero-zero-one, in anticipation of an expected Varkolak armed response for the arrests made earlier today. These images, collected from the Argos telescope at the edge of Sol Sector, reveal what experts say is a massing of the Varkolak Armada near Theta Draconis. A Federation travel advisory is in effect for Sol, Mizar, Denobula, and Tellar Sectors, and Federation citizens are cautioned to—"

Uhura switched off the Federation News Service feed

on the treadmill's viewscreen and tapped the controls, increasing her speed. She wanted to run faster. Farther. To leave all her mistakes behind. Gloomily, though, she realized the treadmill was an apt metaphor for her situation. No matter how fast and how hard she ran, she was still going nowhere.

She glanced at the chronometer on the treadmill. It was almost 1900 hours. Time to see if she could start moving forward again. Uhura shut down the treadmill and stepped off, heading for the showers.

The Varkolak Armada was massing near Theta Draconis, she thought as she got undressed in the changing room. That was right on the border of the Theta Cygni and Tznekethi Sectors, if she remembered her astronavigation classes. She did some quick math. At warp five, the Varkolak could be in Federation space in a matter of days. Sooner if they pushed to maximum warp. There wasn't much time left to put things right.

Uhura went to take a sonic shower, letting it massage the sweat off her. The Academy Sports Complex was fairly empty, with the restrictions put on cadets being out of their dorms, but she wasn't surprised when someone got into the shower stall right next to hers and switched on the sonics. Nor was she surprised when the shadowy figure spoke to her.

"Cadet Uhura. We understand you have something

new for us." It was the same woman who had contacted her before, and told her to steal a Varkolak sniffer. Or the same voice, at least.

"I do," Uhura told her. "It's a Varkolak phaser."

"The Varkolak phaser technology is inferior to ours," the woman told her.

"I know," Uhura told her. "But I thought it might be useful for . . . other purposes."

Uhura let her Graviton contact think about that. If she was the saboteur, she would see the opportunity immediately. If she wasn't . . . Well, it wasn't hard to imagine how a Varkolak phaser could be used to incriminate them, even if it wasn't used for a more violent purpose.

"You're right," the woman said at last. "I'll pass it along. Where is it?"

"Locker four ninety-two. In a satchel."

"Good work, Cadet. Shields up."

"Shields up," Uhura warned the woman as she left her shower stall, and this time Uhura meant it.

Kirk hurried across campus. If he'd been worried at all about the Assassination Game—which he wasn't at the moment—it wouldn't have mattered. The eyes of Starfleet Security officers everywhere. They were posted at the doors to the dorms, the classroom buildings, and the administration buildings. They were patrolling the old parade grounds and the paths around the quad. He got wary looks from a few of them, and one or two told him to hurry along to wherever it was he was supposed to be. But while there were security officers everywhere, the Academy's cadets were noticably absent from the campus. It felt like a proverbial ghost town.

It wasn't just the threat of more attacks. There was a general feeling of foreboding in the air, like at any moment, the public viewscreens around campus would light up with a flashing red alert, calling every cadet into active duty and sending them scrambling for shuttles and transporters. It had happened once before, Kirk knew—some response to a Tholian incursion into Federation space a hundred years ago—and everyone was buzzing that it might be happening again soon.

Kirk was stopped at the door to Nimitz Hall and asked his business there. The security officer finally cleared him, but only after scanning him with a tricorder. Kirk was fairly shocked, but if Bones was under suspicion, he supposed all cadets could be. All the more reason to get Bones cleared, pronto. He took the steps two at a time and punched a door chime.

"Da?" asked a heavily accented Russian voice.

"It's Jim Kirk," he told the intercom.

The door slid open, and the young teenage wunderkind,

Pavel Chekov, met him with a huge smile on his face.

"Welcome!" he said. "What brings you to Nimitz Hall?"

Kirk loved this kid. Just last semester, Kirk had tried to drown Chekov in the kid's own room. Kirk had been infected with a neural code that had hot-wired his brain and made him do things he didn't remember, but still . . . Most people would take something like that personally. Not Chekov. The kid was smiling at him like Kirk was his big brother, and Kirk found he kind of liked that Chekov thought of him that way.

Kirk clapped a hand on his shoulder. "Chekov, I need your help."

"Of course! Yes! Come in!" The young cadet gestured to a pot of something violently reddish purple simmering on a hot plate. It smelled like beets and sour cream. "Would you like some borscht?"

"Um, no, thanks, I just ate," Kirk said. "How did you get a hot plate up to temperature to make soup?"

"What? Oh, I made a few modifications to it. You know what they say, 'You don't own it until you open it.'"

Kirk had never heard that line before, but then again, he and Chekhov didn't exactly run in the same circles. "I need you to tell me who called my roommate's communicator," he said.

Chekov frowned. "Um, forgive me, but can you not just check the call log?"

"We know whose phone it came from, but she says it wasn't her who called. Somebody used some software or something to imitate her voice."

Chekov's eyes went wide. "Oh, yes. I see! Very clever! Very clever! But . . . why is your roommate recording his calls?"

"It got pushed as a Priority One message, just in case he had his phone on standby. Somebody *really* wanted him to wake up and take this call."

"And all Priority One calls are recorded! Yes! It is clear to me now. What is the message?"

Kirk called up the recording and played it for both of them to hear.

"Who the hell calls at two thirty in the—"

"Priority One call from Nadja Luther."

"Leonard? Leonard, it's Nadja."

"Nadja? What's wrong? Why are you calling—"

"Leonard, I need you to meet me at Cavallo Point, right way."

"What? Now? Why?"

"Please, hurry."

"Nadja? What's wrong? Nadja?"

"Priority One call ended."

"It's the girl's voice that's the fake one," Kirk said, just to be clear.

"Oh. Aye. You can hear just a hint of distortion. But it

is a very good mask. Very good indeed."

Kirk couldn't hear any difference in the recorded voice and Nadja's voice at all, but that's why he'd come to Chekov.

"Can you do it? Can you . . . back-mask it, or whatever?"

"Yes. Yes, I think I can. I'll have to run it through an acoustic resonance inverter and then feed the digital file to a sonic parser and then perhaps run a harmonic analysis of—"

Kirk held up a hand. "I knew I came to the right person. Do whatever you have to do."

Kirk's communicator chimed, and he flipped it open.

"Kirk here."

"Jim, it's Nadja. It's Daagen. He's up to something. Can you meet me behind the astrosciences building?"

"I'll be right there," Kirk told her. He snapped his communicator shut and stood. "Sorry. I've gotta run. You'll call me when you've got something? It's kind of urgent. Fate of the galaxy and all that."

"I will get on it right away!" Chekov promised. He grinned, picking up a hyperspanner from the random tools and devices on his desk and spinning it in his fingers. "You don't own it until you open it."

CH.20.30
Dragons, Dog-men, and Ninjas

Daagen was taking a field trip, and Kirk and Nadja were going with him.

He didn't know they were going with him, of course. But when he slipped out the back of the library by the loading dock, to avoid the security officers patrolling the campus, they followed a few minutes later. When he took the nature trail down to the harbor, so did they—fifty meters behind him. And when he took the ferry across the bay to San Francisco, they hopped into a cab to take them over the bridge, to wait for him on the other side.

Nadja threw her backpack in next to Kirk, and they were off.

"What's he doing, going into the city?" Kirk asked.

"Nothing good, I'll wager," Nadja said.

They arrived just after the ferry did, and Kirk spotted

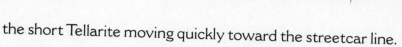

the short Tellarite moving quickly toward the streetcar line.

"Keep the car! Keep the car!" he told Nadja, just as she was paying the fare, and he slid into the back seat. To the driver, he said, "Follow that streetcar!"

Kirk shot Nadja a smile. "I've always wanted to say something like that."

The taxi followed at a discreet distance. Daagen didn't get off the streetcar for a long while, and when he finally did, it was in one of San Francisco's most colorful, vibrant neighborhoods.

"Chinatown," Nadja said.

"Ever been?" Kirk asked.

Nadja shook her head.

"Come on. You're going to love it."

Souvenir shops and small cafés lined the streets just past the Dragon Gate, but soon Daagen turned off onto the side streets of the neighborhood, and the tourist traps gave way to markets with chickens hanging in the windows and restaurants with menus written in Chinese. The sidewalks were full of people, and it wasn't too hard to stay hidden from Daagen, though he did still stop and look around every other street corner or so.

"What do you think he's got in that satchel?" Kirk asked.

"Maybe he's making a dumpling delivery," Nadja suggested. "Or maybe it's empty and he's here to pick up some."

Daagen eventually found where he was going: a warehouse on the outskirts of Chinatown. He punched in a code at the door, took one last look around, and slid inside. Kirk hurried forward to catch the door, but he just missed.

"We'll have to find another way in," Nadja whispered. "There's an open window up there."

"Wait," Kirk said. He started putting in combinations on the door. The light over the keypad blinked red each time he failed. Red. Red. Red. Red.

"Give it up, Kirk. There are ten thousand possible combinations between zero-zero-zero-zero and nine-nine-nine-nine. If we climb up the fire escape and you boost me over, I can—"

The light over the keypad turned green and the door ka-chunked—unlocked.

"Not ten thousand," Kirk told her. "Just twenty-four. The plastic over the keypad is indented over the numbers in the combination. Four numbers, twenty-four possible combinations."

Nadja gave him an impressed look. He put a finger to his lips and opened the door far enough for them to slip inside.

A dragon stared back at them.

It was red and pink, and had a snarling, toothy mouth, like, well, like a Varkolak, Kirk was forced to admit. Stacked beside it were barrels of folded paper umbrellas and piles of red lanterns. Overhead hung yellow fish on poles and a snaking golden dragon with a tail five meters long. The place was a storehouse for Chinese New Year costumes and props of all kinds.

"Happy new year," Nadja whispered.

"Yeah. I think it's the year of the rat," Kirk said. "Let's go catch him."

"Split up," Nadja suggested. She pointed Kirk one way and she went the other.

Kirk threaded his way through hundreds of colorful fans, hung with string from the ceiling, toward a giant tiger head so big, it had to ride on a float. Still no sign of Daagen. Maybe if he got up on top of the tiger head, he could see better—

"Hi-yah!"

A man in a creepy demon-dog mask jumped out from between two dragons, and Kirk jumped back. He was too big to be the Tellarite, which meant he was probably one of his secret-society cronies.

Kirk punched, kicked, jabbed. The big man took the shots well, and he gave Kirk a few in return. After just a few seconds, Kirk decided he could take him, but not without a lengthy fight. And every moment he spent fighting this goon, Daagen was off doing who knew what.

"Sorry," Kirk said. "I've got a date."

He knocked a box of costumes onto the dog-man and kicked him headlong into another pile of lanterns.

It wouldn't keep him, Kirk knew, but it gave him enough time to slip past and take off through the stacks of parade props. Stealth was out now, so Kirk didn't care how much noise he made as he ran. He careened into another dragon head, got his balance back, turned a corner, and ran full tilt into a woman in a Starfleet cadet uniform. They went down together with a collective "oof," the girl landing underneath him.

"Kirk?" Uhura said.

"Uhura?" Kirk said.

"Hi-yah!" said a third person, and he flew into Kirk foot first, kicking him off Uhura. Kirk tumbled painfully into a stack of crates and then pulled himself up. It wasn't the dog-man this time, but someone else, dressed all in black, with a black ninja mask on his head.

"What is *with* this place?" Kirk said aloud.

The man in black shot a look at Uhura on the ground, and Kirk suddenly worried it was Uhura he was after, not Kirk. He looked around wildly for something to use against the ninja and spotted a rope that held a giant panda head suspended right over them. Kirk grabbed the end of the rope and yanked. The knot gave, and the rope hissed up and over a pulley on the ceiling as the panda head came crashing down. Uhura squeaked and tucked into a ball, and the ninja jumped away as the head smashed into the ground, trapping Uhura inside.

"Don't worry, Uhura! You'll be safe inside there!" Kirk called, and he took up a defensive stance against the ninja.

"Hi-yah!" The dog-man crashed into Kirk from behind and knocked him to the ground again, where they fought and kicked among spilled masks. Above them, Kirk saw the ninja hop up onto a pile of crates and then disappear.

"That's right, run away!" Kirk yelled. "I could have taken you bo—*oof*." The dog-man punched him in the gut, and Kirk lost his breath, but he recovered in time to kick his assailant over his shoulder.

"Kirk! Kirk, let me out of here, you idiot!" came Uhura's muffled yell from inside the panda head.

Kirk got back to his feet, but the dog-man was just as quick, lowering his shoulder and driving Kirk back into a door and out into the street beside the warehouse. People scattered as they knocked over a noodle cart. Kirk and the man in the dog mask grappled as someone cried out for the police, and Kirk saw the man pull a knife from his pocket.

"That's dirty pool," Kirk began to say, until he saw what kind of weapon it was the man held. "Wait—a *spork*?"

Kirk ripped the mask off the dog-man. It was Finnegan.

"What the hell?" Kirk said. He headbutted Finnegan

and rolled over on top of him, holding his arms down with his knees. Finnegan? Here? Now? Playing the Assassination Game when there were spies and ninjas everywhere?

Kirk raised a fist to deliver a knockout blow to Finnegan when someone caught his hand. He spun, ready to punch the ninja, but pulled up short.

It was a San Francisco police officer.

"Stand down, Cadet," the officer said. "You're both under arrest."

CH.21.30
The Rules of Engagement

"Ten, Kirk," Admiral Barnett said. "That's ten fights. And this one in a crowded street in Chinatown, of all places, when you're not even supposed to be off campus!"

Kirk felt distinctly like he was sitting in the principal's office back in grade school—a place he had sat many, many times.

Beside him, Jake Finnegan snickered at Kirk's predicament.

"And *you*, Cadet Finnegan!" Barnett said, rounding on him. "I've got a complaint list a kilometer long on you from plebes you've made it your business to bully and terrorize. Believe me, when you graduate—*if* you graduate—I can bury you so deep in space, the only person you'll have to pick on will be your transporter echo. I know a particular ice planet near Vulcan where you're lucky if you see a supply ship once a year."

Rule number one in the principal's office: don't smile. They hate when you smile. Kirk did his best not to smile at

Finnegan getting called to the mat, and then proceeded to initiate rule number two: earnestness and conciliation are your only chance out.

"It was all just a game," Kirk told Barnett. "We weren't *really* fighting." He looked to Finnegan for backup here.

"Uh, no. I mean, he's right. It was just . . . good-natured fun."

Kirk had to swallow his tongue. It was anything but fun for the two of them, of course. However, rekindling their old conflict here in Barnett's office wasn't going to do them any favors.

"A game?" Barnett said. "What game?"

Kirk winced. He'd broken rule number five: don't ever give them something new they can use against you. He shot Finnegan a look of warning, but it was too late.

"The Assassination Game," Finnegan said. "We each got some other cadet's name, see, and we have to track them down and try to kill them with a spork when nobody's looking."

Admiral Barnett raised his considerable bulk out of his chair and leaned forward upon his desk. "Are you telling me you're playing a game like this here? *Now?* With all that's happening with the Varkolak?"

Kirk closed his eyes and waited for it.

"*Have you lost all sense of judgment?* We are about to go to war with the Varkolak. *War,* gentlemen. Not some game. We have had terrorist attacks on Academy grounds. People have *died*. We have Starfleet Security officers posted at every door and at every building, watching for anything suspicious, and you're telling me *you're running around pretending to kill one another with sporks*?"

"The game started before all that," Finnegan said.

"And none of you geniuses ever thought that maybe you should put it on hold when things did get serious?"

Finnegan had no answer for that. None of them did. Kirk had been more focused on the bombings than on the Assassination Game, but he'd still gone after his targets when he had the chance. And he'd still fought to keep Finnegan from knocking him out of the game. Their goose was looking cooked.

Rule number three: When your back is against the wall, change the conversation.

"Admiral, Bones—Cadet McCoy—he's being set up. That's what I was doing in Chinatown in the first place, trying to clear him. There's another cadet, Daagen, a medical student. He's a part of some secret society here at the Academy. I think they had something to do with the bombing. I followed him to Chinatown, where he was making some kind of a drop, but Finnegan here jumped me before I could—"

"Enough! I don't want to hear any more! From this moment on, the game is over. Do you understand? It ends this instant. If I see a spork in either of your hands, anywhere outside the dining hall, so help me Cochrane, I'll have you on a shuttle back to whatever cornfield you came from before you can say 'converter coil.' Do I make myself clear?"

"Yes, sir," they both said at once. That was rule number six: The principal is always right.

"Now get out of here," Barnett said. He slumped back into his chair, closing his eyes and massaging the bridge of his nose. Kirk and Finnegan didn't have to be told twice. They'd both been in enough principals' offices to know to run when you could.

Out in the hall, Jake Finnegan punched Kirk on the shoulder, hard.

"See ya around, Jimmy boy," Finnegan said, and as he walked away, Kirk knew that for Finnegan, the Assassination Game would not be over until Kirk was dead.

Uhura stood outside the door to Spock's staff apartment, hesitating before she rang the chime. She'd never been to Spock's room before. They had always met somewhere else: the observation tower, the faculty cafeteria, the racquetball court. When he'd told her to meet him here, at his apartment . . . Well, if he were human, she'd take that as something more than it was. But Spock wasn't human, she reminded herself. Meeting here was no different than meeting in the stellar cartography lab. She took a deep breath and rang the chime.

"Come in," Spock said.

The door whisked open, and Uhura stepped into the most spartan living space she'd ever seen. There was little else in the room besides a table and two chairs, and the small kitchen along the far wall was so clean and tidy, it looked like he hadn't even moved in yet. The only personal touches to the room were a small painting on the wall of some place on Vulcan, with its three suns on the horizon; a 3-D chess set on the table; and in the corner, on a pedestal all its own, a Vulcan lute. The last surprised Uhura; she had no idea Spock was musical.

Beyond where Spock was standing, hands behind his back, was the door to what she guessed was his bedroom. Not that she would ever see it.

"Cadet Uhura, welcome," Spock said. "May I offer you some refreshment?"

"No," Uhura told him. "I'd hate for you to have to take anything from its place."

Spock raised an eyebrow, but said nothing more. Uhura went to the table to look at the chess set.

"You're in the middle of a game," she said.

"Always," Spock said.

"Who are you playing?"

Spock almost looked embarrassed, if Vulcans could be embarrassed. "Myself," he said. "I rarely have visitors. You are the second, actually."

"Oh, you have another 'special relationship'?" Uhura asked, trying to keep the bitterness out of her voice.

Again with the eyebrow. "No," Spock said. "I do not."

Uhura was almost touched by that, but she reminded herself that a special relationship meant something very different for Spock than it did for her.

"Were you able to ascertain who Cadet Daagen delivered the phaser to?" Spock asked.

There we go, Uhura thought. *Back to business.* After handing the Varkolak phaser off to her contact, they'd been able to track it as the weapon passed through three different pairs of hands. They'd discovered Daagen, a medical cadet, had been the latest. It wasn't a real Varkolak phaser, of course. Spock had built a remarkable facsimile of one, aided by the fact that Varkolak phaser technology was actually slightly behind that of the Federation. A Varkolak sniffer—even a modest knockoff of one—was well beyond his capabilities.

"No," Uhura told him. "I followed the tracer you put in it to Chinatown, and I was all set to record the handoff when this cadet I know, Kirk, dropped a panda head on me."

That one scored her highest hit yet on the Spock eyebrow meter.

"Don't ask. Suffice to say, I missed the handoff. I didn't see who got it."

Spock nodded thoughtfully. "We shall have to rely on the tracer inside it, then. At best, we may have only missed an opportunity to out yet another member of the Graviton Society."

"And at worst?"

"At worst, the rogue agent within the society now has the device, and we will not know who the person is until he or she moves to use it again."

"We need more eyes and ears," Uhura said.

"I have thought so from the beginning," Spock told her. "Cadet Sulu, I believe it is time for you and Cadet Uhura to become acquainted."

The door to Spock's bedroom opened, and Hikaru Sulu joined them. Uhura was stunned. Had he been in there the whole time? But of course he had. Uhura looked back and forth between Spock and Sulu, feeling like the world's biggest fool.

"We've met," Uhura said sourly.

"Indeed," Spock said. "Two cadets were nominated for inclusion in the Graviton Society at the same time: you and Cadet Sulu. I worried even then that I was under suspicion by the hierarchy of the Graviton Society and that my recommendation of you would be seen for what it was: an attempt to bring in more 'eyes and ears,' as you call it. I therefore approached Cadet Sulu with an offer: Should he be uninterested in joining the Graviton Society to further its stated goals, perhaps he would join to further mine."

"I was kind of interested in joining," Sulu said bashfully. "I thought being part of some elite fraternity would help me get to where I want to go in Starfleet, but I was also afraid it might just be a distraction, something that wasn't really part of my plan. I spoke to Commander Spock about it after I was officially invited but before I'd given them my answer. He convinced me to say yes."

"And become a double agent for him," Uhura said.

"Precisely," Spock said. "Once they trusted Cadet Sulu, I would then have advance warning of any attempts to expose the two of us as infiltrators. And, in fact, his very first assignment from the society was in that regard."

"The plot to drive the Varkolak off Earth with the transmitter," Uhura said, understanding now. "It was a fake."

Sulu nodded. "They thought you might be in league with Commander Spock, so they sent me to feed you false information. I'm sorry. I couldn't tell you what I was doing. I told Spock, though."

"You knew already?" Uhura asked. "And you didn't tell me?"

"Yes. I hid Cadet Sulu's role from you, so as not to compromise his position should they use him in another such attempt to expose me. It was vital they not see you as anything but a willing member of the society."

"Was stealing the Varkolak sniffer another test, then?" Uhura asked.

"It is unclear," Spock said. "But I think not. I think, rather, it was initiated by the rogue agent within the Graviton Society, passing the command along to her subordinates on the chain of command, as though the order had come from the top. Then, when you acquired the device and sent it back up the line, that person kept it for his or her own secret purposes."

"And now they may have it, and I missed the handoff," Uhura said.

"You didn't miss much," Sulu told her. "The person who picked it up was cloaked."

"You saw it? You were there? In the warehouse?" Uhura asked. Then she understood. "The ninja! The ninja who kicked Kirk! That was you!"

Sulu smiled sheepishly. "I'm hardly a ninja. But, yes, that was me in disguise. I followed you at Commander Spock's request, to be an extra pair of eyes and ears, but then that cadet attacked you, and I—"

Uhura laughed out loud. She couldn't help it. Both men looked at her strangely. "I'm sorry," she told them. "Kirk didn't attack me. The idiot just ran into me. He was as surprised to see me there as I was to see him there."

"Yes. I didn't know who he was or what he was doing there, but when the man in the dog mask attacked him, I backed off, not wanting to get into any fight I didn't understand."

"This other cadet, Kirk," Spock said. "Could he be a member of the Graviton Society?"

"No," Uhura told them. "Trust me. He's not."

"I'm sorry I kicked him, then," Sulu said.

"Oh no," Uhura said. "Don't worry about that. He totally deserves it."

"Regardless," Spock said. "We still have the means to track the phaser's movement, and there are now three of us to keep watch. You have the tracking program on your PADDs. The phaser is currently hidden in the basement of Yi Sun-Sin Hall. When the person who placed it there retrieves it, the program will alert us. It is imperative we converge on the person at once, in case he or she is the rogue agent. Agreed?"

"Yeah," Uhura said. "And let's just hope it moves again before the Varkolak reach Sector zero-zero-one."

"Indeed," Spock said. "Thank you both."

"Um, can I walk you back to your dorm, Uhura?" Sulu asked.

Uhura was a bit taken aback. She hardly needed an escort across campus, but Sulu knew that. Unlike Spock, for whom there was never any subtext, Sulu had to mean that he was interested in her and wanted the pleasure of her company on the way back. She liked Sulu—what she knew of him—but then there was Spock. . . . But what was she waiting around on Spock for? It's not like he was going to sprout emotions overnight and start serenading her on his lute.

"I—" Uhura began, but Spock interrupted her.

"I need Cadet Uhura to stay behind so I might to speak to her," he said. "Privately."

Uhura was surprised again. If she wasn't so sure he didn't care, she would have thought Spock had said it just to keep her from spending quality time with another man.

"Oh, all right," Sulu said. To Uhura, he said, "Another time then." He said his good-byes.

Uhura crossed her arms and leaned against the table, sure that Spock had some new mission for her. Some game within a game that, like the 3-D chess set behind her, he was playing against an imaginary opponent.

"Cadet Uhura," Spock began. He frowned. "Nyota. What I have to tell you is not easy for me."

Uhura got a weird feeling. Spock? Uneasy about telling her something? If they had been dating, she would have thought he was about to break up with her.

"I have been giving a great deal of thought to our con- versations of late—particularly those in which I argued for the Graviton Society. Or at least those in which I advocated a harder line for Starfleet. From the beginning, you argued that trust, loyalty, and honor were the hallmarks of Starfleet, emotional intangibles that I dismissed in favor of logic. But I see now that you were correct. I apologize."

Uhura didn't know what to say.

"You don't—you don't have to apologize to me, Spock."

"I believe I do. Despite your help in the past to become more . . . emotionally intuitive . . . I am still largely ignorant of the nuances of human behavior. Especially when it comes to relationships. Even so, only a Pakled would fail to understand that this mission has strained our relationship, and that was never my intention. In fact, quite the opposite is true: I asked you to participate not only because you were qualified for the role, but because, selfishly, I wished to spend more time with you."

Uhura's heart was thumping in her chest. She had felt this way about him all along, thought that he was spending more time with her and sharing more of himself with her than anyone else because perhaps he felt the same way about her that she did about him. But he was Vulcan. He didn't allow himself emotions. And this mission, the Graviton Society—all of it. He was right. It had come between them. Shown her just how *alien* he was. But if she was honest with herself, the reason she was so mad at him was because she had realized, finally, that she was in love with him. She crossed to the corner where Spock's lute stood, mostly so she could hide the warring emotions in her face.

"I thought that's what we had, Spock," she told him, still not looking at him. "I thought we had a . . . a 'special relationship.' But then everything started to change."

Spock came up close behind her, but didn't touch her. "The fault is mine, Nyota. I have been reviewing the series of decisions that allowed me to deem what the Graviton Society was doing as acceptable, and I have come to the conclusion that I relied too heavily upon logic. As I did with our . . . special relationship."

Uhura almost turned, but she could hear Spock's voice change as he looked away. He was opening up to her now, opening up in a way he had never done with her before. Perhaps, she thought, remembering his embarrassment at playing chess alone, perhaps opening up in a way he had never done with *anyone*.

"When I was a boy growing up on Vulcan, I was constantly bullied by those who sought to remind me of my human half. As if they would ever let me forget. In my subsequent efforts to prove to them, and to myself, that I am a Vulcan, I ignored the fact that humans have many admirable qualities. Some," he said meaningfully, "even more than others. Of all your admirable qualities, Nyota, I find your heart to be your most admirable, and it pains me to think that through my own ineptitude, I have lost it. It is my sincere hope that you will continue to share it with me and to help me remember to sometimes be . . . more human."

Tears rolled down Uhura's face, and she touched the Vulcan lute in the corner. She had thought Spock could never drop his logical exterior and serenade her, and yet he just had.

"Would you like to hear me play it?" Spock asked, seeing her hand on the lute.

Uhura turned. "Not tonight," she told him, and she pulled his head to hers and kissed him.

CH.22.30
Sucker Punch

Uhura wasn't answering her communicator. Kirk had tried calling her all evening, but she was avoiding him. First, she had stolen the Varkolak sniffer and told him it was to take down a secret society. Then she'd sat there and let Lartal be accused of bombing the medical conference when she knew someone else had done it. Then when he and Nadja had followed Daagen to Chinatown, there she'd been, hiding out behind some barrels of wobbly headed dolls with a holo-camera. Kirk wanted answers from Uhura, and he wanted them *now*.

It was already late at night when the security officer at the door to Uhura's dorm gave him the okay to go in. Kirk had told him he was there to visit a lady friend, which was techincally true—although not in the way he led the officer to believe. It got Kirk inside, though, and he found Uhura's door and rang the chime.

"It's Kirk," he said. "Open up."

The door did open, bit it wasn't Uhura standing there. It was Gaila, Uhura's curvy, red-headed, green-skinned Orion roommate.

In her underwear.

"Hey, Jim," she said with a smile.

"Um, hi, Gaila," Kirk said. Orion women had some kind of pheromone that sped up the metabolisms in most men, and Kirk could already feel his heart racing. Or maybe it was the push-up bra. Either way, he had to force himself to stay on task. "I'm looking for Uhura."

"Oh, pooh," Gaila said, giving him a fake pout.

"Is she here?"

"No. I think she's spending the night out. And Uhura *never* spends the night out." She played with the zipper at the top of Kirk's uniform. "But that means I'm all alone, in case you're looking for someplace to spend the night."

Every molecule of Kirk's body was screaming for him to step inside, close the door, and not come out until next week.

"That . . . is a tempting offer," he forced himself to say. "But I'm going to have to take a rain check. You have no idea where Uhura is?"

"Nope," Gaila said, looking up at him with come-hither eyes.

"All right," Kirk said. "I'll just—I'll have to—I'm going to go look for her somewhere else."

Kirk stayed right where he was. Gaila smiled.

"Right now," Kirk said.

Gaila backed into her room, inviting him to follow her. Kirk put his hands on the door frame, trying to hold his feet back from taking him inside. It took every ounce of will-power he had, but he broke away and ran off down the hall.

"Good night, Gaila!" he yelled.

"Come back later, Jim," she called after him. "I'll be waiting."

Kirk slumped to the floor of the turbolift, breathing heavily and wishing he could take a *very* high-pitched sonic shower right now. But that too would have to wait.

"Bones, I hope you know what kind of sacrifices I'm making for you, buddy."

Desperate to find something, *anything* that would help clear his best friend, Kirk took a long walk in the dark to Cavallo Point. Cadets had seen him leave his dorm, so maybe someone had seen where he went. It was a long shot, Kirk knew, but it was all he had. That, and the cool night air helped clear his head from his run in with Gaila.

But Cavallo Point was as quiet and empty that night as it had been when Bones had come here, at least according to what Bones had said. Kirk took awhile to wander the park, listening to the low undertone of the ocean waves from far down the cliff. Who had called Bones out here, pretending to be Nadja? Who wanted him to take the fall for contaminating the shuttle debris with kemocite to implicate the Varkolak? And what was that rustling in the bushes?

Kirk stopped, and the rustling stopped.

"Who's there?" he called.

Nobody answered.

Kirk went into the bushes where he'd heard the sound and then pulled out his communicator, using it to illuminate the ground at his feet.

Four big round eyes blinked back up at him. It was two Tarsian men in Starfleet uniforms. Or, at least, *mostly* in Starfleet uniforms. They hastily zipped their tunics back up as they shielded their large eyes from the light.

"Whoa. Hey," Kirk said.

"You mind killing the light?" one of them asked.

"Oh. Sure. Sorry," Kirk said. Tarsians were nocturnal, and had enormous black eyes that were the size of grapefruits. Their big eyes were disconcerting, but Kirk figured his comparatively little eyes must be weird for them.

"What are you guys doing out here?" Kirk asked.

"Um . . . stargazing," one of the cadets said.

Right, Kirk thought. *Stupid question.* "Come here often?" he asked.

"Look, pal, this is a *monogamous* relationship. If you're looking to hook up with someone, I suggest you try the Warp Core. Or maybe the Delta Quadrant."

"No, I mean—" Kirk sighed. This wasn't going right. "No, I mean, seriously, do you come here often? Like, were you here three nights ago? It's important. I'm trying to help a friend." He explained everything to the two cadets, who had their clothes back on and were sitting up now.

"The grumpy cadet? Yeah, sure. I remember him. He kept calling out a girl's name," one of them said.

"But there wasn't anyone else here. Except us. And we just laid low until he was gone."

"He took off after a while, still grouching."

"That's him! Yes!" Kirk said. "Can you guys come back with me right now and tell that to Admiral Barnett?"

"Admiral Barnett? Now?" one of the Tarsians said. "Why? Does it matter?"

"Oh, yeah," said Kirk. "It matters."

It was morning by the time the Tarsians stumbled sleepily back to their dorms to go to bed, but their testimony was enough to spring Bones. There was still the not-so-insignificant matter of the kemocite found in their room, but until Starfleet could prove where and when Bones had acquired it, or that it was used to make the explosive that took out the president's shuttle, McCoy was a free man.

"It's not like I ever had a motive for any of this, anyway,"

Bones groused, making sure the security officers working the brig heard him. Kirk hurried him away.

"*Probation,*" Bones muttered as they walked. "As though I did any of this."

"Don't worry, Bones. We'll get you cleared." He told Bones all about how he and Nadja followed Daagen into Chinatown, even though neither of them, it turned out, had been able to catch Daagen red-handed.

Bones clapped him on the shoulder. "Thanks, Jim. I owe you one."

"You owe me *two,*" he said, meaning Gaila, but he didn't elaborate. "Coming back to the dorm?"

Bones shook his head. "Somebody I want to see first."

Kirk smiled. He meant Nadja, of course. A brand-new relationship, with all the fun and perks that come with it, and he'd spent one of his first nights in the brig. "Right," said Kirk. "Say hello to her for me. She's been a big help, by the way. She's the one who spotted Daagen headed off campus in the first place. I think she really likes you, Bones."

Bones grinned, then thanked him again, and they parted ways.

Kirk thought about heading back to his room for that overdue sonic shower, but it was breakfast time already and he was starved. He'd eat first, then shower, then sack out in bed. Without any classes to get to—

Somebody sucker punched Kirk in the kidneys, and he stumbled and then fell.

"Hey, Jimmy boy."

"Finnegan," Kirk spat. The big cadet had him all alone, and Kirk sighed. As much as he loved the idea of the Assassination Game, the admiral was right. This just wasn't the time or place for it. Kirk dragged himself to his feet and held his hands out in submission.

"All right, Finnegan. You win. Spork me. I'm out."

Finnegan snarled. "I'd love to, Jimmy boy, but I can't."

"What? Why not?"

"I'm out," Finnegan told him. "I got bumped off walking back to the dorm from Barnett's office. Now somebody else has a spork with your name on it."

"I don't suppose you'd tell me who it is."

Finnegan laughed. "Not a chance." He took a step closer, his hands clenched into fists.

"Whoa! I thought you said you were out," Kirk said.

"Just because I'm out of the Assassination Game doesn't mean I'm not gonna kill you, Jimmy boy."

Kirk had finally had enough. Without the game to worry about, without a spork to dodge, he attacked without fear. In thirty seconds, Finnegan was laying in the grass with one hand clutching his bloody nose and the other grabbing his busted knee.

"Barnett's right, Finnegan. You're nothing but a bully."

Finnegan spat blood at him, but missed. Kirk grabbed Finnegan by the collar and raised a fist, threatening to punch him again.

"Tell me something, Finnegan. How did you know to be waiting on me in Chinatown?"

Finnegan laughed, despite his pain. "Your girlfriend told me you were going to be there."

Kirk frowned. "My girlfriend?" He wasn't dating anybody right then. Not for more than a night or two, at least.

"That girl you were with. The leggy one who runs the game. She sold you out, Kirk. She was the one who told me you were going to be there."

Kirk shoved Finnegan away and left him wallowing on the ground. He'd just gotten one answer to this mess, and now he had more questions. Why would Nadja go to such lengths to eliminate Kirk from the Assassination Game? With everything else that was going on?

But the better question was, how did Nadja know they were going to end up in that warehouse in Chinatown?

CH.23.30
Secrets Within Secrets

Kirk was right: McCoy's first stop wasn't his dorm room. It was Nadja's dorm room. A night in the brig was hardly the best way to follow up on what had been a promising start to a relationship. A very promising start.

In fact, it was the most promising start he could remember since his ex-wife.

McCoy tried to put the implications of that away as he checked in with the guard at the entrance to Nadja's dorm and then took the turbolift up to her floor. He would have called first, but Kirk still had his communicator, checking into whoever had left him that message in the middle of the night. When they figured that out, McCoy figured, he'd be free and clear for good—and they would have some idea about who was really behind all this. For his money, it was Daagen, and by all rights, the Tellarite should have been the first person McCoy had gone to confront. But there was that incredible night under the stars on the Argos telescope with Nadja that he couldn't forget, and he had a good chance for a repeat performance if he played his "you're the first person I wanted to see when I got out of jail" card right.

Nadja's roommate, a Brazilian cadet named Beatriz, was the only one in their room when McCoy got there, though.

"She swapped duty with somebody on the telescope," Beatriz told him.

"Really? They're still running telescope duty when classes are canceled?"

Beatriz shrugged. "Now more than ever."

This was good, McCoy thought as he left. No, better than good. This was perfect! What better way to reprise the other night than with an encore performance?

A quick sonic shower and a change of clothes later, McCoy caught a shuttle up to McKinley Station and hitched a ride with a Starfleet transport shuttle to the Argos telescope. They warned him they weren't due back for a pickup run for the cadet on duty for another four hours, and McCoy tried to keep a straight face as he told them he would survive.

McCoy went through the umbilical hatch and into the station bearing a picnic basket and a bottle of wine, but Nadja wasn't in the control room.

"Hello?" McCoy called.

No answer. He left the picnic basket and the wine in the control room and went into the labyrinth of corridors that wound in and around the giant space telescope's machinery. He finally found Nadja's back end sticking out of a Jefferies tube on level four.

"Nice view," he said.

Nadja jumped as much as the crawl space allowed her and fell out of the Jefferies tube, pointing a laser welder at him.

"Whoa," McCoy said. He put up his hands in mock surrender. "Sorry to surprise you. Who were you expecting, the Varkolak?"

Nadja relaxed and put down the laser welder. "No. I— Sorry. You startled me. I thought I was alone. What are you doing here?"

"Got out of jail, and you were the first person I wanted to see."

"Oh. Right. I'm glad you're out."

McCoy had hoped for a bit warmer reception than that, but she was probably still recovering from the release of epinephrine from her adrenal glands, which his shock had given her.

"Come on. I've got a bottle of wine and a picnic basket waiting back in the control room," McCoy told her.

"Let me just get my things," she said. She pulled a tool bag from the Jefferies tube and sealed it back up.

"What were you working on?"

"Nothing important. A faulty ODN relay. Thought I'd save the SCE a trip to install a few feet of new conduit. You know, they charge you by the hour," she joked. She slipped an arm through McCoy's. "Come on. Let's go celebrate your release from captivity."

Secrets within secrets within secrets. Kirk was so tired of chasing shadows. But how could he get a straight answer out of anyone when he couldn't find them? He'd tried Uhura's communicator all day, but she was clearly avoiding him—and there was no way he was going to chance going back to her dorm room to look for her. Resisting Gaila's charms *twice* in one week would be impossible, even for a Vulcan.

So when Kirk saw Daagen in the Academy dining hall that afternoon, he decided he was done playing games. He marched right up to the table where Daagen sat with two human cadets.

"You. Daagen," Kirk said. "It's time to talk."

The Tellarite turned his pig nose up at him. "I know you," he said. "I knitted your leg bone back together. If you've come for a checkup, I'm on call at 1600 hours."

"I know all about your little secret society, Daagen."

Two cadets from the next table over turned to look.

Daagen smiled and poked at what was left of his lunch with a spork.

"I'm sure I don't know what you're talking about," he said.

Kirk planted both hands on the table so forcefully, it rattled their trays and made their drinks slosh. Daagen's two buddies slid out their chairs and stood menacingly, but Daagen waved them back into their seats.

"No need for any more spectacle than there already is," he told them. They sat, and Daagen smiled up at Kirk. "Have I done something to offend you, Cadet . . . Kirk, was it?"

"You're messing with my friend. Leonard McCoy. Maybe you've heard of him."

"Oh, yes. Unfortunately. You're right if you think I dislike him. But I'm not 'messing with him,' as you put it. Nor are any of my friends," he said cagily.

"You mean your Graviton Society buddies," Kirk said. He honestly didn't know much more than that, but that little nugget had made Daagen's buddies squirm. The Tellarite was made of sterner stuff, though.

"Again, neither I nor any of my fellow cadets have attempted in any way to interfere with Dr. McCoy. It is he who has been interfering with us."

"Because you're trying to start a war between the Federation and the Varkolak. Because you're hurting innocent people."

"Please," Daagen said.

"You stole Nadja Luther's communicator and used it to get rid of Bones, so you could use his password and taint the evidence to point the finger for the shuttle explosion at the Varkolak."

"I was in space that night. On duty at the Argos telescope. You can look it up."

"Fine. One of your minions, then," Kirk said. "You set up Bones, in case Starfleet discovered what you'd done, to put the suspicion on him. When that didn't work, you set another bomb, using that Varkolak sniffer."

"What Varkolak sniffer?" Daagen asked, all trace of humor gone.

"That scanning device you had stolen from them. You used it as the detonator on that bomb at the conference, to pin it on the Varkolak. To drag us into a war. What I want to know is, why?"

Daagen stood. Even hunched over the table, Kirk was still taller than the Tellarite.

"Are you saying Starfleet has *evidence* of Varkolak involvement in the second explosion, and they haven't said so?"

"You know damn well they do, because you put it there!" Kirk told him. But he was beginning to have his doubts even as he said it. Daagen was no longer staring at him defiantly. Instead, his quick, dark eyes looked this way and that as he absorbed what Kirk was telling him. Kirk suddenly worried he'd been wrong—and that he'd just given this stupid secret society insider information Starfleet Security was obviously looking to keep under wraps.

"This is very interesting news," Daagen said. "Very interesting, indeed."

"It's not news. Not to you, Daagen."

"Oh, but it is, I assure you, Cadet Kirk. And very interesting news, indeed. Something that should be shared with the Federation News Service, I think. Don't you? After all, if we're about to go to war with the Varkolak, we ought to know why."

Kirk had been a fool. He saw that now. If Daagen and his group had planted the Varkolak sniffer, they wouldn't have waited for Starfleet to announce a Varkolak device had been recovered. They would have leaked it to the interplanetary news services right away. Just like they were about to do right now.

"You *didn't* plant that bomb, did you?" Kirk said.

"You've told me the truth, Kirk—a very valuable truth. So let me share one of my own. My friends and I," he said, clearly meaning the Graviton Society, but without truly acknowledging their existence, "believe in the Federation. We love it, and we want to see it prosper. We would never do *anything* that would harm it, or any of its citizens—no matter how misguided they are. We want a stronger Federation, Mr. Kirk. Not a weaker one. And now I think I shall go and strengthen it considerably by rallying it against a common foe."

Daagen's buddies got up, smiling, and they left the dining hall. Kirk sat at their table, thinking it all over. He'd been so sure Daagen was behind all this. Bones had been so sure too. But Daagen's argument made sense. And when the story about the Varkolak sniffer hit the news within the hour, it would prove Daagen hadn't known about the sniffer in the first place. If he had, why sit on the story? Daagen was a jerk, and his stupid secret society was a joke, but Kirk believed him when he said he hadn't engineered any of this. But if not him, who?

Across the dining hall, Kirk spotted Braxim, the big Xannon cadet. He was just finishing sweeping the last of his lunch into the recycling bins. Kirk felt the Starfleet badge in his pocket—the one with Braxim's name on it—and snatched up a spork from Daagen's tray. He'd had bigger things to worry about lately, but when opportunity came knocking, you didn't ignore it.

Kirk hurried after Braxim and caught up with him on the sidewalk back to the dorms. Alone.

"Brax! Hey, Brax, buddy. You forgot your spork."

"Huh? But the spork I used belongs in the—"

Kirk tapped the spork to Braxim's chest, and the big Xannon's eyes grew wide, understanding. He laughed, bellowing so loud, Kirk was sure they could hear him across the bay in San Francisco.

"Excellent!" Braxim said. "Most excellent! I was very close, I think, but you have bested me. I yield, sir." Braxim pounded his chest the way Xannons liked to do, smiling. That was one of the reasons Kirk liked Braxim so much. To the big guy, everything about life was entertaining, even getting beat—which, admittedly, didn't happen very often for him. But Braxim was just about the best sport in the galaxy.

"Here," he said. He pulled another cadet's badge out of his pocket and gave it to Kirk. "I wish you all success. I have not been able to track my target down, despite two days with no classes. She's always sneaking off some place."

Kirk took a look at the name, then grinned. Winning this was going to be easier than he thought.

Kirk's communicator chimed, and he flipped it open. It was Chekov. He had something.

"I'll be right there," Kirk told him. "I've gotta go, Brax. Buy you a drink later at the Warp Core?"

"I accept!" the big Xannon said, and he walked off, shaking his head and laughing.

●　·　✦　∴　✦　·　✦　·· ·

"What have you got for me?" Kirk asked.

Chekov was excited. Geeked out, you might say. Whatever he had, Kirk knew it was big.

"It took me some time, but I was able to reverse master the message," Chekov told him. He sat down at the computer in his room, where ten different windows were open with equalizers and graphs and strings of numbers.

"So, you can prove someone scrambled their own voice to sound like Nadja Luther?"

"Oh yes. It was very advanced work, too," he said, butchering his Vs. Kirk tried not to smile. "To work backward, I actually isolated the baseline and ran it through a modified version of the universal translator. Then I ported it back through a—"

Kirk waved him off. "Chekov, cut to the chase."

Chekov frowned, not understanding.

"Just play it."

"Oh! Yes. All right." Chekov tapped his screen, and the same message played again in Nadja Luther's voice.

"No, not the masked one," Kirk told him. "I want to hear the original one. The one you *un*masked."

Chekov was practically bouncing in his seat. "That *is* the one I unmasked." Kirk didn't quite understand what the young cadet was saying, and Chekov clarified it for him. "This *is* the original. This is what was first recorded and then scrambled."

"But . . . but that's Nadja's voice. It sounds just like the message left on Bones's communicator."

"Not exactly, but close enough to fool him into thinking it was her voice, yes."

"It was Nadja?"

"Yes! With just enough digital noise to make somebody like me *think* it was someone else's voice being masked. It is a very clever piece of engineering."

Kirk sat back on Chekov's bed. Nadja Luther used a voice masker to hide the fact that she was using her own voice? Nadja had left the message on McCoy's communicator, then denied it to his face? But why?

There was only one reason Kirk could think of, and he didn't like it. But the more and more he thought about it, the pieces began to fit together. He pulled the badge he'd won off Braxim out of his pocket. What was it Braxim just told him? *I haven't been able to track her down. She's always sneaking off someplace.* He flipped it over and read the name on the back again: Nadja Luther. Nadja Luther, who'd been sneaking around. Nadja Luther, who'd been pulling Bones's strings.

Nadja Luther, who'd been orchestrating everything from the very beginning.

CH.24.30
Red Alert

"Let's be frank here," said Captain Littlejohn. "We may be looking at the end of the Academy."

Littlejohn's statement was met with a great deal of muttering and open dissent around the faculty table. Spock, as usual in these unnecessarily contentious faculty meetings, held his tongue.

"Preposterous," said Professor Usarn, an Illyrian. "The end of the Academy? This institution has existed for almost a hundred years, and it survived worse crises than this."

"All I'm saying," Littlejohn said over a new round of arguing, "*all I'm saying* is that when we go to war with the Varkolak, we're not going to have the luxury of training cadets. They'll be thrown into service on starships as soon as they sign up."

"*If* we go to war," said Captain Martinez.

"If? If, Captain?" said Commander Naan. "Have you

seen the latest feeds? The explosion at the medical conference's opening was detonated with a Varkolak device! It must be war!"

Spock had seen the FNS news feed just before the faculty meeting. The word that a Varkolak scanning device had been used to trigger the explosion was finally out, though it did not sound as though the announcement had come from Starfleet itself. A leak, then. Spock had too little information to hypothesize who had released the information, but he certainly knew whose cause it would help: the Graviton Society.

Talk around the table turned to the Varkolak device and then to a heated debate over the definition and appropriate application of the term "circumstantial evidence," which the Academy's instructors attacked with the kind of dogged zeal only a room full of academicians could muster. Ordinarily, Spock would have enjoyed the course of the debate, but at that moment, he was more interested in an alert that had just popped up on his PADD.

The object was on the move.

"Come on, Spock," Captain Shimada said. "You're too quiet over there. Back me up on this one."

"I beg your pardon, but I must be excused," Spock told the assembled faculty. He stood, gathering his things to a stunned silence. His departure was unprecedented, he knew. He alone had never missed a single second of faculty meetings in all his time at the Academy. The amazement over his departure was short-lived, though. By the time he reached the door, they were arguing among themselves again, oblivious to his absence.

In the hallway just outside, Spock flipped open his communicator. "Cadet Uhura, the object is on the move," he said.

After a moment, Uhura answered, "Spock! Sulu and I are already on it."

"I'm outside Yi Sun-Sin Hall," Sulu said, joining in on the communication. "I see someone. It has to be her. She's moving in the same direction as the tracking signal."

"Cadet Uhura, do you have a visual?" Spock said. After the night they had spent together, it was difficult not to use her first name when speaking to her, but decorum was required.

"I'm almost there. Wait— Yes. I have her now."

"Do you recognize her?"

"Negative. She's a cadet, that much is clear, but I don't know her name. I'm sending you a picture."

Within seconds, the picture appeared on Spock's PADD.

"She is a senior cadet by the name of Nadja Luther," Spock told them. He saw almost every cadet at some time or another in the simulations, and of course he remembered them all.

"Is she the one?" Sulu asked. "Or is she just delivering it to someone else?"

Before Spock could answer, klaxons blared in the hallways and classrooms, accompanied by flashing red lights. A campus-wide emergency. The screen of his PADD immediately filled with an official emergency broadcast signal, heralded briefly by the light blue–and–white logo of the United Federation of Planets. The logo blinked away and was replaced by the head and shoulders of Admiral Barnett.

"Cadets and faculty, may I have your attention. I have just received word that the Varkolak Armada has entered Sector zero-zero-one. All Starfleet ships in the area are rendezvousing to intercept. Starfleet reserve officers are hereby recalled to active duty, and cadets are ordered to report to shuttle hangers and transport stations for assignment at once. The Federation is mobilizing for war."

The Academy faculty spilled out of the classroom where they were meeting, and the hallway erupted into chaos. As they ran past, talking and shouting, Spock finally answered Sulu's question.

"I do not know, Cadet. But we may have run out of time."

Bones was digging through the pile of clothes in his closet when Kirk came running into their dorm room.

"Bones! Bones, it's war. We have to report to the transporters."

"I know! Why do you think I'm rooting around in here for my damn blue tunic? I'm not going to show up looking like a first-year plebe in an Academy uniform. Aha!"

Bones came up with a blue shirt that would identify him as a doctor, and sniffed at it. He recoiled at the smell, but still stripped out of his Academy reds and pulled it on.

"Here," Kirk said. He tossed Bones back his communicator.

"You're done with it? Did you figure anything about about my mystery caller?"

"Yeah," Kirk said. How in the world was he going to tell Bones about Nadja Luther? He had to. He knew that. But that didn't mean it was going to be any fun. Instead, he yanked out his gold command-division tunic and pulled it on over his black undershirt.

"It was Daagen, wasn't it?" Bones said. "The little devil."

"No," Kirk said. "It wasn't Daagen."

Bones waited for Kirk to go on, but Kirk pretended to be looking for something.

"Well?" Bones said. "Don't leave me in suspense, man! Who was it?"

Kirk sighed. No sense putting it off any longer.

"It was Nadja."

"What?"

"Look, Bones, I'm sorry, but it's not Daagen or anybody

else who's been messing with you all this time. It's Nadja."

"You're crazy."

"No, Bones. I know you don't want to know this, but just listen, all right? The message on your phone? The call you got that night you went out to Cavallo Point? It's Nadja's voice, scrambled, then modulated to sound like her voice again."

"But why on earth would—"

Kirk held up a hand. "That first night you went on a date, that night you went for a walk with her dog in the park. You told me she showed up at the research lab and told you you were late, even though you could swear you weren't."

"So?"

"So, when you left, was she with you when you said your access code to the computer?"

Bones sat down on his bed, his eyes seeing another time and another place.

"Bones, Nadja planted that kemocite on the shuttle. She was there, on the dais, remember? She set it up not to hurt anybody, but she caused the explosion. She's an engineer. She knows better than anybody what kemocite and plasma do when they come together. But she also knew all the kemocite would be consumed in the chain reaction, so she used a recording of your access code to sneak back into the lab and contaminate the shuttle debris.

She probably had a recorder in her purse when you said your access code. She *wanted* Starfleet to point the finger at the Varkolak. But just in case her sabotage was discovered, she set you up to take the fall for it by sending you on that wild goose chase to Cavallo Point. She thought no one would see you. You'd be seen leaving the dorm late at night, but nobody would see where you went. You'd have no alibi in the investigation. She contaminated the shuttle debris with kemocite while you were gone, then left her communicator on Daagen's desk and claimed she'd lost it. It was misdirection. Daagen didn't have anything to do with it at all."

"You're guessing," Bones said. "It's all conjecture. That message from Nadja—someone's done something clever with it to mix us up. And what about the kemocite planted in my closet?"

"Nadja spent the night with you here one night, didn't she? That night I was gone?"

Bones turned pale.

"Did she stop by her room first?" Kirk asked quietly, trying to soften the blow. "Did she bring anything with her?"

"She said—she said she just needed to get her tooth-brush," Bones said.

"But she brought an overnight bag with her or something, didn't she?" Kirk said.

Bones nodded.

"The kemocite had to be in it. I'm sorry, Bones, but the whole time, she was setting you up in case she got found out. And . . . there's more."

"More?"

"When you were in the brig, Nadja and I followed Daagen to Chinatown. She's the one who saw him go."

"That doesn't mean anything."

"No. But, Bones, Jake Finnegan was there. He attacked me. Kept me from seeing whoever it was Daagen was there to meet. I couldn't figure out how Finnegan knew to be waiting for me in Chinatown when *I* had no idea where we were going. *She* told him. Nadja. Finnegan says she told him to be at that warehouse in Chinatown to attack me. But how did *she* know where we were going? The only answer is that she was the one there to meet Daagen."

"You're saying she's a member of this secret society."

"I think so. But I don't think even Daagen knows what she's up to. Not by the way he reacted when I told him some of this stuff."

"But why?" Bones asked. The pain was clearly written on his face now. "Why blow things up, why hurt people, *kill* people, and make it look like the Varkolak did it?"

"Before the red alert sounded, I was in the library," Kirk told him. "I looked up Nadja's public record. Her parents were killed on Vega V when the Varkolak attacked."

Bones closed his eyes. "Of course. Damn it, why didn't

I see that? She told me she grew up on Vega colony and that she came back to Earth when her parents died. But I never made the connection with the Battle of Vega V."

"It has to be a revenge thing, Bones. That's what all this is about. It's why the entire Federation is about to go to war with the Varkolak. Because of her."

Bones was silent for a time, and Kirk felt the insistent urging of the flashing red-alert message on their room console. They had to get going.

"Bones?"

"It . . . it all fits, I have to admit," he said at last. "I just . . . I need to talk to her, Jim."

Kirk offered a hand to help up his friend. "That is definitely step one."

CH.25.30
Charmed Lives

McCoy and Kirk arrived on the Constitution-class USS *Potemkin's* transporter pad in a tornado of swirling subatomic particles. When the transport was complete, McCoy patted himself down to make sure all his limbs were intact and where they were supposed to be.

"Don't worry, Bones. You're all there. Physically, at least," Kirk told him.

"Laugh now, Jim, but one day you're gonna come through that thing with an extra arm sticking out of your chest and then who's going to be laughing?"

"Jake Finnegan, I'd expect," said Kirk.

The other Academy cadets who'd transferred with them filed off the transporter pad to check in with a Denobulan yeoman who stood by the door handing out assignments.

"I'm Yeoman Phozic. Welcome to the USS *Potemkin*, Cadets. Names?" he said when Kirk and Bones reached him.

"Kirk, James Tiberius, and McCoy, Leonard Horatio," Kirk told him. "But what I really need to know is where a cadet named Nadja Luther is posted."

Phozic tapped his PADD. "Weapons room . . . and sickbay."

"You mean she's in one of those places? Here?" Kirk asked.

"No. James T. Kirk, field rank lieutenant, you're to report to the weapons room. Leonard H. McCoy, field rank lieutenant commander, you're to report to sickbay. You're the last group to report in. Hurry to your stations."

"No, we need—Wait a minute, you outrank me?" Kirk said to McCoy.

"That's 'You outrank me, *sir*,'" McCoy corrected.

Kirk turned back to Phozic. "Look, we need to know where Cadet Nadja Luther ended up. It's important. *Please.*"

"Cadet, this is no time to be worrying about where your girlfriend ended up."

"She's not his girlfriend, she's mine. And finding her may be the only way we can stop this war from happening. Now look her up, Yeoman. That's an order," said McCoy.

Yeoman Phozic seemed to understand all at once that McCoy did, in fact, outrank him, despite the differences in their ages.

Kirk gave McCoy an impressed look as Yeoman Phozic hurriedly tapped at his PADD.

"Luther, Nadja. She was assigned to the *Farragut*, but . . . it says here she didn't report for duty. She's listed as AWOL. The *Farragut* warped out without her."

Kirk leaned over the transporter console and clicked the intercom button. The transporter chief started to object, but Kirk cut him off.

"Captain Mitchell, this is Cadet Kirk. I've got some information that could stop this war with the Varkolak before it even begins. There's another cadet, her name is Nadja Luther, and she's a part of a secret society at school. She blew up the president's shuttle, and she set off that bomb at the medical conference and made it look like the Varkolak did it, all because her parents died in the Varkolak attack on Vega V. She's still on Earth, and she's getting away."

There was a pause, and the four men in the transporter room held their breaths. Finally, the captain's slightly put-out voice came back to them through the comm.

"This is all very fascinating Cadet . . . Kirk, is it? But this isn't the time. In case you hadn't heard, there is an alien armada headed for Earth, and the *Potemkin* is a ship of the line, and belongs with the defense fleet. Now close this channel and report to your station!"

McCoy saw that Kirk was about to talk back and hauled him out into the corridor.

"But, Bones!" Kirk protested.

"Let it go, Jim. He's not interested. You heard him. The armada's on the way. The talking is over. Everybody's ready for war. How did you know who the captain was, anyway?"

"I know all the captains in the fleet. Who's this ship's chief medical officer?"

"Dr. Thomas Arnet."

"See? You know your business, I know mine."

Kirk steered them down a side corridor of the ship.

"Wait a minute? Where are we going? The turbolift's that way."

"You're not going to sickbay, Bones, and I'm not going to the weapons room. We're going back down to Earth."

McCoy pulled Kirk to a stop. *"Are you out of your confounded mind?* They're never going to let us transport down."

"I know. We're going to steal a shuttle," Kirk said, moving off again.

"Oh. Good. I thought we were going to do something stupid."

"Nadja's behind all this, Bones. If we warp out of here with the fleet, there'll be a war. She'll have gotten exactly what she wanted, and she'll have gotten away with it too. If we catch her in time, maybe we can put everything right before the shooting starts."

"Jim, the deck officer isn't going to let us—" McCoy lowered his voice as they passed a *Potemkin* crewman in the hall. "He isn't going to let us just waltz into a shuttlebay and borrow one for a joyride."

"Probably not. I don't suppose you've got a hypospray on you, do you?"

"Oh, sure. I just walk around with a hypospray filled with anesthezine, in case I have to knock out somebody."

"Do you?"

McCoy turned and gave Kirk a look that said a very exasperated "no."

"Well, I hate to do it, then, but I'll probably have to fight him. Just . . . be ready to run."

"Fantastic."

The door to the shuttlebay whisked open ahead of them, and McCoy took a deep breath. What they were about to do would either end up getting them a commendation or landing them in the brig. Or maybe both.

The deck officer had his back to them as he moved crates onto a hoversled. Kirk put a finger to his lips and snuck up behind him. He tapped the officer on the shoulder and raised a fist, ready to strike—then stopped suddenly when the officer turned.

"Leslie!"

"Kirk? What are you doing here?" Leslie asked. He frowned at the punch Kirk had been about to throw him.

"Bones, this is my friend Leslie. He and I fought the Varkolak. Before that, we were furniture together."

McCoy had no idea what Kirk was talking about, but he let it go. They might get out of this without a fight yet.

"Leslie, we need a favor," Kirk told him. "A big favor."

Kirk laid it all out for him as quickly as he could. Nadja, the secret society, the explosions, the sabotage, the wrongful imprisonment of the Varkolak. "We've got to go after her, Leslie. And for that, we need a shuttle."

Leslie looked queasy, then straightened. "You know, I just remembered," Leslie said. "I . . . have to go to the bathroom."

"Thanks, Leslie. You're a pal," Kirk told him.

"The *Indomitable* is prepped and ready to go," Leslie said, walking away. "And I never saw you."

Kirk and McCoy hurried over to the shuttlecraft *Indomitable*. "And you said no one was going to let us waltz out of here with a shuttlecraft," Kirk said. He had the door closed and the shuttle lifting off in moments.

"We lead charmed lives, Jim. Charmed lives," McCoy told him.

The *Indomitable* passed through the *Potemkin*'s shuttle-bay's force field and into the black of space, and Kirk steered it toward Earth.

"Shuttlecraft *Indomitable*, this is Captain Mitchell of the USS *Potemkin*," the intercom blared, making them both jump. "This is an unauthorized departure. Return to the shuttlebay immediately."

"I hereby retract my comment about us leading charmed lives," Bones said.

Kirk clicked a button. "I'm sorry. I can't do that, Captain. Nadja Luther's still on Earth, and if we can catch her—"

"Cadet Kirk! If you do this, your career is over. Do you understand? You won't just be kicked out of the Academy. You'll be court-martialed for going AWOL during a state of war. I'm giving you one last chance. Turn that shuttle around *now* and get back to the Potemkin."

Kirk clicked off the transmission and kept flying for Earth.

"Don't worry," he said. "I've studied all the captains in Starfleet. I know their MOs. Mitchell's going to let us go. Just watch."

The shuttle rocked as the *Potemkin* opened fire on them with its phasers.

"Or not!" cried Kirk.

CH.26.30
Any Landing You Can Walk Away From

The Academy grounds were chaos. Cadets ran to and from dorms, pulling on uniforms as they reported to transporter rooms and shuttlepads. Instructors ran with them, shouting orders and reporting for duty themselves. Shuttles lifted off over trees in the distance, heading up into space and across the bay to the Presidio, where Starfleet Command was located. Announcements and news reports blared from every console and public viewscreen.

Uhura and Sulu met Spock in the shadow of the statue of Admiral David Farragut in the middle of campus. All of them had their PADDs in hand, watching the movement of the tracer hidden in the replica Varkolak phaser Spock had constructed.

"It's still moving," Uhura said.

"Do we intercept?" Sulu asked.

"It would be better if we could first see what the cadet intends to do with the device," Spock replied.

"Catch her red-handed," Uhura said.

"If I understand the colloquialism, yes. That would be ideal," Spock confirmed.

Right about now, Uhura began to appreciate Spock's calm under pressure. She wouldn't want to live without emotions all the time, but there were definitely moments she wished she could switch them off, like a chip in her head that could be deactivated.

Spock tapped at his PADD. "As an Academy commander, I have the authority to reassign you. Cadet Uhura, you have been assigned to the communication pool on the USS *Lexington*. Cadet Sulu"—he tapped again and raised an eyebrow at what he saw—"Cadet Sulu, you have been assigned as the relief helm officer aboard the USS *Excalibur*. A well-deserved posting, if I might add."

Sulu looked stunned. Uhura was too. Relief helm officer was a big deal for a cadet right out of the Academy, let alone one still *in* the Academy.

"Relief helm? On the *Excalibur*? She's a Constitution class," Sulu said with wonder. He shook himself out of it. "But I'll stay here, of course. This cadet has to be stopped."

"Your dedication to duty is admirable, Cadet Sulu," Spock said. "But your duty as a helm officer on a ship of the line takes precedence. I am releasing Cadet Uhura from her assignment, but not you. There is a shuttle leaving for McKinley Station in thirteen minutes and twenty-seven seconds from shuttlepad six."

"Are you sure?" Sulu asked, already backing away.

"Quite certain, Cadet," Spock told him. "I sincerely hope events do not require you to replace the *Excalibur*'s helm officer, but if they do, pilot well."

"I will, Commander. I will!" Sulu called, taking off for shuttlepad six at a run.

Uhura wheeled on Spock, her ponytail whipping behind her. "What am I, chopped liver?" she demanded.

Spock frowned.

"You release me from duty and not Sulu? I know he's good at what he does, but so am I!"

Spock seemed to understand at last.

"Indeed," said Spock. "You are the finest linguistics student at the Academy. But if we fail to apprehend Nadja Luther and convince Starfleet *and* the Varkolak of her complicity in these events, Cadet Sulu's talents will, unfortunately, be in much greater demand. Stay with Luther. Follow the signal. That she is transporting the device in the midst of a crisis is telling."

"Wait, you're not coming with me?"

"While I have the authority to change your assignment, I do not have the authority to countermand my own. For that, I will first need to speak to my watch commander."

"Forget your watch commander, Spock! Just come with me! This is more important!"

Spock raised an eyebrow, still cool as could be. "Go AWOL? In the middle of a crisis? No. Without obedience to the hierarchy of command, we would have chaos. I will go through the proper channels and, if successful, I will join you. If I am denied, I will take my assigned post on the USS *Intrepid*."

Uhura wanted to growl. Spock was too damn rigid for his own good sometimes! This was one of those times when some human emotion and initiative would be better than his Vulcan logic.

"But, Spock, what if—"

"I assure you, Nyota, you are more than capable of doing this alone, if need be. I have absolute faith in your abilities—and in you."

Uhura got butterflies in her chest. For someone who could occasionally say the absolute wrong thing, Spock had a strange knack for every now and then saying the absolute *right* thing. She stood on her toes and gave him a quick kiss.

"I won't let you down," she told him, and she ran off to follow the signal.

● · · ✦ ⋮ ✦ · ✦ ·· ·

Smoke filled the shuttle's small cabin. Sparks flew from the navigation console. Kirk did everything he could to keep the pitch of the *Indomitable*'s nose up and not bring them down in the middle of San Francisco harbor—or worse, on top of the Golden Gate Bridge—but the shuttle was on its last legs after the pounding Captain Mitchell and the *Potemkin* had given it.

"You have a serious problem with authority figures, do you know that, Jim?" Bones told him.

"Physician, heal thyself."

"I'm trying to, damn it!" Bones had been caught when one of the consoles exploded. He was trying to treat the burn with the shuttle's med-kit, but he couldn't aim straight. "Keep it steady, why don't you!"

"Tell that to the port thrusters that went out five minutes ago!"

Kirk wrestled the thrusters under control and alerted shuttlepad four's deck officer of their imminent emergency landing. One of the landing struts crumpled under them as they hit, and the shuttle skidded along the tarmac, but Kirk and Bones were able to hang on without being thrown. When the shuttle finally came to a stop, they sat where they were for a moment, waiting to see if anything else would explode.

"Well, any landing you can walk away from, eh, Bones?"

Bones looked ashen. "That's it. I quit Starfleet. I don't care if my ex-wife *is* somewhere on Earth. It's a big place. A big place that doesn't *move*."

Kirk slapped his friend on the shoulder. "Come on, Bones. You don't have to quit. They're going to court-martial us out."

"Speaking of," Bones said. He nodded through the viewscreen, where a group of redshirted officers were hurrying their way. "Are they engineers or security?"

"They really need to have different colors for different jobs!" Kirk said.

They hurried to the shuttle's door and pulled up when they found a redshirted officer already waiting for them.

"Wow," he said. The outside of the shuttle was burned and scarred from where the *Potemkin*'s phasers had punched through their shields. "Have you already seen action with the Varkolak?"

"Not exactly," Bones told him.

The other redshirts were drawing nearer. "You there! Hold on!" one of them called.

"Got to get a message to the admiral!" Kirk lied, and he and Bones took off at a run.

Their first stop was Nadja Luther's dorm room, for lack of a better place to start. Bones figured if she was getting away, she'd want to take some of her things with her. If it was Kirk, he would have just legged it, but then he had never been too possessive of his stuff.

The dorm was empty. The lobby, the turbolifts, the hallways. Everyone else was on their starships, warping off to meet the Varkolak. Kirk wanted to be with them out there. It was what he had trained for. Why he had joined Starfleet to begin with. But Starfleet was a "peacekeeping and humanitarian armada." That's what Captain Pike had told him that night back in Iowa when he'd talked Kirk into joining up. And what better way to keep the peace than to stop a war before it began?

Kirk was imagining the medal he would get for this when he turned the corner and walked straight into Uhura. They went down in a tangle of arms and legs, the PADD she was holding skittering away on the floor.

"Kirk!"

"Uhura!"

"McCoy," Bones said, waving hello.

"What are you *doing* here, Kirk?" Uhura demanded.

"What are *you* doing here?"

Uhura didn't answer. Instead she tried to get up, but she and Kirk were still too tangled for either of them to get free.

"*Grr.* Kirk, why is it, wherever I go, you end up on top of me?" Uhura asked.

"Just lucky, I guess," Kirk said with a smile.

The door beside them slid open, and a startled Nadja Luther stared back at them, a satchel slung over her shoulder.

"Nadja!" Bones said.

"Leonard?"

"Kirk!" yelled Uhura.

"Uhura—" said Kirk.

"Mrs. Penelope, *greif an*!"

Nadja's little cairn terrier shot from the apartment and latched onto Bones's pant leg, growling and tearing.

"Ow! Down, you little devil! Heel! Halt! Desist!"

Nadja barreled past them, knocking Bones into Kirk and Uhura and sprinting down the hall.

Bones righted himself and kicked his leg out, flinging the little terrier harmlessly down the hallway. "Come on!" he said, dragging Kirk to his feet. "Before that holy terror gets its legs back!"

"Sorry!" Kirk said over his shoulder to Uhura as Mrs. Penelope went after her instead.

Nadja had grabbed the only turbolift, so they took the stairs. She was already out the door and halfway across the quad before they got outside, but Kirk was able to close the gap on her while Bones lagged behind. At first Kirk thought she might be heading for a transporter, but she took a left at the public transporter hub and ran for one of the shuttlepads. Kirk knew if she got there before he caught up to her, they would lose her. Nadja's long legs and athletic training kept her out front. She blew past a stunned deck officer at the shuttlepad and threw herself into the only shuttle left, a short range Class F called the *Davy Crockett*. The door lowered shut just as Kirk got there, and he leaned on it and banged on the duranium hull.

"Nadja! Stop! Wait!"

She wasn't about to do either one. Kirk heard the shuttle's ion engine fire up, and he backed away as the shuttle lifted off and swung around, heading up into the atmosphere.

Bones ran up, panting. Uhura was right behind him.

"Now we've lost her!" she said. "Damn it, Kirk! You've ruined everything!"

"Me? I'm not the one who was skulking around in what was supposed to be an empty hallway."

"I was *skulking*, as you call it, because I was trying to stop the person who planted those bombs!"

"Nadja Luther," Kirk said. "Yeah. We know. That's what we were doing there too."

The confused deck officer ran up, checking her own PADD. "That cadet can't just take a shuttle without filing a flight plan," she said. "Where's she going?"

Kirk shook his head. "No telling."

Uhura checked her PADD and shook her head. "I've lost her. She's out of range."

"No," Bones said, trying to catch his breath. "No, wait. I know where she's going."

Kirk, Uhura, and the deck officer all waited impatiently for him to get his wind back.

"Spit it out!" Uhura told him.

"Not all of us joined Starfleet because we like to run all over creation," Bones groused.

"Bones, where'd she go?" Kirk asked.

His friend sighed. "The Argos telescope. I'd bet the horse farm on it."

"Argos?" Uhura said. "Why?"

"I caught her rooting around in the machinery the last time I was there. She told me she was just fixing something, but . . ."

"We need a shuttle," Kirk told the deck officer. "It's an emergency. That woman, she's the one who planted the bombs at the medical conference, and now she's headed for the Argos telescope."

"W-What?" the deck officer stammered. "But—"

"We don't have time to explain," Uhura told her. "Please. We need a shuttle."

"That was the last of mine," the deck officer said. She checked her PADD. "There are still shuttles at pads one, three, six, and nine, but they all have cadets on them for transport to McKinley. They'll be leaving any minute."

Think, Kirk told himself. *Think. You don't have a shuttle. How do you get to Argos?*

"Wait! Can I see that?" he asked the deck officer. She shrugged, handing him her PADD. He scrolled through the passenger manifests. *Please, please, please—Yes! There!*

"Hold this shuttle!" he told the deck officer. "Tell them . . . tell them there's turbulence, or something's wrong with their antimatter containment, or there are turtles on the runway—something. *Anything.* Just don't let them take off yet!"

"All—all right," the deck officer said, bewildered.

"Kirk, they're never going to let us have one of those," Bones said.

Kirk shook his head. "We don't need a shuttle. We've got something better." He took out his communicator and flipped it open.

"Kirk to Chekov; come in, buddy."

CH.27.30
The Hitchhiker's Guide to Starfleet

Pavel Andreievich Chekov waited for his transport shuttle to lift off, clinging to his personal safety harness in exactly the way the instructional vid told them to. He didn't care that all the other cadets around him weren't paying attention to the vid or holding on in the correct fashion; it wasn't an order, after all, just a recommendation. And it wasn't that he didn't trust the shuttle or had any doubts about the pilots. It was just that there were reasons for doing things the right way. In this case, holding on would help prevent minor bumps and abrasions should they experience turbulence in the atmosphere or loose artificial gravity in space, which had been known to happen.

The safety vid ended, and Chekov took a deep breath and relaxed, trying not to think about his assignment. It was important not to get too excited. Getting excited made him look like he was a kid, which he practically was, but he wanted—he *needed*—his senior officers to think of him as an adult. In less than an hour he'd be standing by as the relief navigator on the USS *Nautilus*, an important posting for the Academy's youngest cadet.

Just telling himself not to get excited got him excited, though. *Calm thoughts*, he reminded himself. *Breathe*. Taking his Vulcan mathematics teacher's advice, he began to recite pi in his head to focus himself. *3.14159265358979323846264643383*—

Chekov's communicator rang.

At first he just stared at his pocket, not understanding. Who did he know who would call him in the middle of a red alert?

Alex Leigh, one of the many twentysomething women in his dorm who looked upon the teenage Pavel Chekov like a little brother, sat beside him on the shuttle. She nudged him.

"Your communicator's ringing."

"Who do I know who would call me in the middle of a red alert?"

"Why don't you answer it and find out?"

Chekov let go of the safety harness, all worries about turbulence and weightlessness tossed aside. He fished out his communicator and flipped it open.

"Who do I know who would call me in the middle of a

red alert?" he asked. "Oh! Hello! . . . You are? She is? You do? Yes—yes, I can do that. I can do that! I'll be right there."

Chekov flipped his communicator closed and unbuckled himself.

"Pavel, what are you doing?" Alex asked him. "We're just about to take off."

"I can't go. They need my help!"

"Who needs your help?"

A redshirted officer came down the narrow aisle of seats. "Cadet, refasten your safety harness. We're getting ready to leave." At the other end of the shuttle, the outer door began to close.

"No! No, wait! I have to get off the shuttle!" Chekov broke for the door, his runner's instincts kicking in and his thin, nimble legs dancing between the outstretched legs of his fellow cadets.

"Cadet! Come back here!" the redshirt called. "You leave this ship and you're AWOL!"

Chekov glanced back in time to see the big officer stumble and fall at the feet of the other cadets, thanks to a trip from Alex.

"Oops," she said. "Sorry, sir." She winked at Chekov, and he blushed and nodded his thanks before diving out through the closing door.

● ˙ ˙ ✛ ˙˙ ✦ ● ˙ ✦ ˙˙ ●

McCoy paced the engineering building's transporter room, wondering what Kirk was playing at. There was no way they could transport up to the Argos telescope from here. Not directly. It was hundreds of thousands of kilometers away, well outside the range of any standard transporter. He kept telling McCoy to be patient, but every second they wasted was another second Nadja Luther had to do whatever it was she had started that night he'd joined her on the Argos telescope.

"We're wasting time," McCoy said again, and again Kirk told him to calm down. His friend was actually leaning casually against the transporter console, like he was doing nothing more urgent than waiting on a pizza to be delivered.

Across the room, Uhura flipped her communicator closed. She'd been talking to someone, filling them in on everything after they had all compared notes, but she hadn't wanted McCoy and Kirk listening in. Secrets within secrets within damn secrets.

"All right. How are we doing this?" Uhura asked. "We're wasting time."

"That's what I keep trying to tell him," McCoy said.

"You guys relax. We can't do this without—and there he is!"

A slight, curly headed, red-faced cadet came running into the room, smiling.

"Here I am!" he said. "I made it!"

Kirk ruffled the boy's hair. "You made great time, buddy. Thanks for coming."

"I am glad to help!"

"Wait a minute," McCoy said. "This kid? Aren't you the one who runs around barefoot all the time?"

"Yes. I find that the foot's natural arch acts as a spring, absorbing the shock of striking the ground and converting the energy of the fall into forward motion, like this," the kid said, demonstrating.

"Well, it's true that running on the balls of your feet remove stress from the plantar fascia," McCoy said. "There's a study of the human foot in the latest—"

Kirk tapped an imaginary chronometer on his wrist. "Um, Bones? Maybe we can table this fascinating discussion for another time?" Kirk turned to Chekov. "We need to get to Argos. You think you can do it?"

"I'm sure I can," Chekov said. He hurried behind the transporter console and began tapping at the controls.

"There's just no way," McCoy said. "The distances are too great. And if you think I'm letting him shoot my atoms off into space in the hopes that they land somewhere—"

"McKinley to *Excalibur*, to . . . the USS *Prester John*, to the USS *Surprise*, if she's still holding station by then . . . then Jupiter Station, back to the *Tennessee*—"

"Wait. You're going to bounce us there, pad to pad?"

McCoy said. "It can't be done, Jim!"

"You did it, Bones," Kirk said.

"Not in five minutes! It took me a week to set up that stunt!"

"You went to Argos by transporter?" Uhura asked.

"To impress Nadja Luther," Kirk told her. "For their big date under the stars."

"Wait, you're *dating* this girl?" Uhura said.

"*Was* dating her," McCoy corrected. "I'd say things started to go downhill when she tried to frame me for treason."

"Later," Kirk said, hustling them up onto the transporter pad. "You can override all the pads you need from here to there?" he asked Chekov.

"I think so."

"He thinks so?" McCoy said. He tried to get back down off the pad, but Kirk held him where he was. "Jim, I had my first drink before that boy was even *born*!"

"You've got enough transporters to get us there?" Uhura asked.

"Um, mostly," Chekov said.

"Mostly?" Kirk said, his grip on McCoy loosening.

"Initiating transport in three . . . two . . . one . . ." Chekov said, and McCoy felt that awful tug in his gut that said he was being broken down into atoms.

He just hoped the junior space cadet could put him back together in one piece somewhere.

Kirk, Bones, and Uhura rematerialized on the familiar small transporter pad of the Argos telescope and stumbled off, trying to regain their senses.

"Hell's bells, how many transporter pads *was* that?" Bones said. He began his usual routine of patting himself down and looking for misplaced pieces.

"I counted eleven," Uhura said. She looked a little sick herself.

Kirk glanced at Bones. "I think that last one might have been the *Potemkin*. I recognized that transporter chief. I hope he didn't recognize *us*."

Uhura pulled out her PADD and tapped it. "The signal! It's here!"

"Well, looks like we didn't take the trip for nothing. Good call, Bones."

"Yeah, I'm ecstatic," he said.

"All right. She's probably trying to set a bomb using the fake Varkolak phaser you gave her," Kirk told Uhura. He took the PADD from her. "Bones and I will take care of Nadja and the bomb."

"What? Why?" Uhura said. She yanked the PADD back from him.

"Because," Kirk said, taking the PADD back again, "*you need to get to the telescope's communication array and tell* the fleets not to fight, and you're the only person here who speaks Varkolak."

Uhura frowned, but she knew he was right.

"Detach her shuttle so she can't get away," Kirk called as he and Bones set off at a run. "And don't worry. We've got everything covered. Trust me!"

"Right," Uhura muttered.

Back in the engineering building's transporter room, Chekov pulled his hands away from the console and smiled.

"I did it," he said out loud to the empty room. "I did it!"

To his surprise, one of the Academy's instructors ran into the room. Commander Spock, from the simulation room. Chekov instinctively stood at attention.

Spock raised an eyebrow. "Cadet Chekov. Should you not be on a shuttle to McKinley Station right now?"

"I—" Chekov began, not sure how to explain his presence here.

"Never mind. I will deal with it when I return," Spock told him. "Stand aside. I need to see if it is possible to transport myself to the Argos telescope." Chekov held up a finger to stop him. "I can do that."

CH.28.30
The Dogs of War

Kirk had Uhura's PADD and the tracking signal to help them find Nadja, but McCoy knew where she would be: in the Jefferies tube where he'd found her before. Replacing an ODN conduit, she'd told him. He'd been such a fool. Love did that to you, McCoy thought. Made you blind, made you deaf, made you stupid. Maybe those Vulcan bastards who denied themselves emotions had it right after all. But then McCoy wouldn't have gotten to feel the righteous anger he was feeling right now, which felt pretty damn satisfying.

Nadja was just climbing out of the access tunnel when they caught up to her. She was as surprised as last time to see them, but this time she leveled a Federation-issue phaser at them.

Kirk and McCoy pulled up to a stop. "I don't suppose you've got a phaser on you, do you Jim?"

"Yeah. Sure. I carry one around so I can stun people whenever I want to."

Touché, thought McCoy, and he and Kirk put their hands in the air.

"That's right," Nadja said, backing away. "You just stand right there."

"Nadja, wait," McCoy said. "Let's talk. There's nowhere to go, anyway. We set your shuttle adrift." *Or we hope Uhura has*, he thought.

Nadja's eyes darted between them, trying to figure out if they were lying.

"We know what you're doing, Nadja," Kirk told her. "You planted a bomb in there with the Varkolak phaser to make it look like the Varkolak did it. It's not a real one, though. It's a fake. People are on to you."

Nadja shrugged. "Doesn't matter, anyway. Once this telescope goes up, the Federation will blame the Varkolak, and before anybody knows any different, we'll be at war."

"How could you do this?" McCoy said. "How could you do this to *me*?"

Nadja shrugged again. "I knew they'd bring the fragments back to your lab for analysis. I needed someone's codes to get in and contaminate the evidence with kemocite. And somebody I could lay it all off on if they figured it out."

"You *used* me," McCoy said. He could feel his right supraorbital vein bulging on his forehead. "Played me like a cheap fiddle, right from the start. You were never interested in me at all. It was always about your little vendetta against the Varkolak."

"The Varkolak are dogs!" Nadja said. There was a wild look in her eye, and her hand shook. Kirk took a half-step forward, but Nadja jerked the phaser back up at him. From where McCoy stood, he could see that the phaser was set to stun, but with a bomb about to go off, the stun setting might be as deadly as the kill setting.

"Starfleet has been too conciliatory. The Varkolak push, and we give. They push more, we give more. You know what happens when you let your dog win a game of tug-of-war with you? They start thinking they're the alpha dog, and you're some whelp. Then they'll never listen to you. Never take another order. We need to show the Varkolak who their master is. One good stare down, one good lesson, and they'll heel."

"The Varkolak aren't dogs, and they're not animals," Kirk told her. "I've gotten to know one. They're people, just like us. Sure, they're a lot hairier and they shed all over the furniture, but—"

Nadja fired the phaser, a blue bolt of stun energy erupting between them in the small corridor. Kirk pushed McCoy out of the way, but part of the blast still hit him in the arm. He spun and fell.

"Bones!" Kirk cried.

Nadja had already turned the corner and was running away. McCoy wasn't unconscious. The stun blast had just glanced his left arm, but his nerves and his muscles were numb and useless. It felt like he *had* no left arm. He grimaced at the weird feeling.

"Bones, you gonna be all right?" Kirk asked.

"Yes, yes. Go. Get her," he said.

Kirk stood and ran. "Defuse that bomb!" he called over his shoulder.

"And just how am I supposed to do that? I'm a doctor, damn it, not a—" he started to say, but Kirk was already long gone. "Oh, never mind."

In the Argos command center, Uhura found where Nadja's shuttle was docked and disengaged the station's locking clamps, setting it adrift. They might want that shuttle at some point, she thought, but it was safer that none of them could reach it. Once they caught Nadja Luther, they could just wait for a starship to come and pick them all up.

If they caught Nadja Luther.

And if all the starships weren't already at war. Uhura had to trust Kirk could put his action where his mouth was and let it go. They had a job to do, and so did she. She retrained the telescope on the Varkolak Armada and gasped at the image that came up on the viewscreen.

More Varkolak ships than she could count hung in the black of space, facing off against an equally formidable line of Federation starships. They weren't shooting yet, but when they did, the carnage would be incredible—on both sides.

Uhura heard someone running in behind her and turned. Spock! She stood and gave him a quick hug and a kiss.

"Where is Nadja Luther?" he asked.

"She's being taken care of," Uhura told him. *I hope.* "I was just about to try and contact the Varkolak. You contact the fleet."

Spock nodded, and without another word, they both set to their tasks.

On the bridge of the USS *Excalibur*, all eyes were on the viewscreen, where the biggest starship armada the quadrant had ever seen arrayed itself in a wide semicircle. The Varkolak. Among the most feared warriors in all the galaxy. And soon the *Excalibur* would be flying straight into the wolves' teeth.

Sulu tried to keep his mind on his job and to not stare at the screen. While the primary helm officer would be flying the ship in, Sulu would be his second pair of eyes, feeding him telemetry on the rest of the ships in their theater of the battle. It wasn't necessary work—one officer could pilot a starship without an assist from secondary helm—but when they had people to spare, every little bit helped. And this way, Sulu would be on the bridge to step in for Lieutenant Bunch if he, well, if he were no longer able to perform his duties.

Ever since he was a boy, it had been Sulu's dream to be on the bridge of a Federation starship. Now here he was. On a Constitution class, no less. One of the lead ships of the Federation's defense fleet. He had dreamed of being here, and he had worked his tail off for it. He had *earned* it, all by keeping his head down and sticking to The Plan. He wished it could be under better circumstances, but he would do his duty to the Federation, in peace or in war.

"Captain, Priority One signal coming in from . . . from the Argos telescope, sir," Lieutenant Chang said.

That pulled everyone's attention away from the viewscreen for a moment. Captain Prax turned in his chair.

"The Argos telescope?"

"Yes, sir. It's from a commander Spock."

Sulu perked up. Spock? Sending a Priority One signal? Had they caught Nadja Luther?

Chang put a hand to the communications bud in his ear and frowned. "He's—he's insisting that the Federation fleet stand down, sir."

"*Stand down? Does the man know we've got a dozen Varkolak target locks on us?*"

"Sir!" cried Bunch at helm. "Varkolak Armada changing position."

"They're advancing, weapons hot!" said Larkin at tactical.

"Helm, take us in. Full power to forward shields. Ready phasers," Captain Prax ordered.

Sulu spun back to his station, hands poised above his console to begin feeding Bunch the extra information he would need, but he paused.

Keep your head down, Sulu. Stay on course. That's what got you here.

But that might not be what would get him out again. Him and the thousand other people on the *Excalibur*, and the thousands of other people in ships on both sides. He took a deep breath and turned.

"Captain, you need to listen to Commander Spock's message," he said.

The senior officers on the bridge turned to look at the field-promoted cadet, like he had suddenly sprouted white fur and grown a rhinoceros horn out the top of his head. All around them, lights were flashing and alarms were sounding, but for the moment, they only had eyes for him.

"I do, Mr. . . . ?"

"Sulu, sir. Hikaru Sulu." Sulu tried hard not to let his voice crack. "Sir, we're about to fight the Varkolak for no good reason. It's all been a plot by someone on Earth, and Commander Spock has been tracking down the truth. You need to listen to him, sir. It could stop a war before it starts."

The captain stared at him for what seemed like an eternity.

"I wouldn't be a very good captain if I didn't listen to my bridge crew," he said at last. "Helm, hold station. Tactical, keep a target lock." He looked at Sulu, though he spoke to the communications officer. "Mr. Chang, let's hear what all the fuss is about."

Nadja Luther moved like a cat through the Argos station's tiny, winding corridors, crawling, climbing, dropping down chutes. Just when Kirk thought he was gaining on her, she would turn and fight back at him, keeping him at bay. But if she wasn't going for her shuttle, where *was* she going? He scanned the station's layout in his mind as he ran. Every one of the cadets had roamed this tiny little station while on telescope duty, looking for anything to distract them from the tedium of staring at consoles for hours on end. There wasn't much to the station, though. Just the optical array, the communications array, the power core, the life-support systems, the shuttle locks, and—

The escape pods. Of course. How could he have been so stupid? There were two of them, tiny things that couldn't hold more than four people apiece, and that uncomfortably, but the station had them, nonetheless. And that's where Nadja was headed.

Nadja fired another phaser bolt at him, and the wall beside him exploded in sparks. He noticed now the blasts were coming in red and not blue.

Nadja had switched from stun to kill.

Kirk saw the station's layout in his head, remembered the tunnels and Jefferies tubes, and ducked off to the right as Nadja went straight. His corridor would cut her off, but without a phaser, what good would it do him? Kirk scanned the ceilings and walls for something he could use and then saw it. He turned the corner, and there was Nadja, coming right for him. She jumped back and raised her phaser. Kirk leaped and grabbed one of the pipes that lined the ceiling—with warnings and exclamation marks all over it—and yanked it apart.

The corridor erupted in a greenish-brown gas, making Nadja cry out and step back. Plasma coolant. Which, besides keeping plasma temperatures in line, would also pretty neatly liquify any organic matter on contact. Kirk opened another pipe facing the corridor he'd come down, cutting off Nadja's route and setting off flashing red lights and computer warnings.

"Give it up, Nadja!" Kirk called through the cloud of coolant. "If you want to live, you're going to have to go back and turn off that bomb."

"Then I'll die, Kirk," she called back. "Why not? I should have died when I was a girl."

"With your mother and father? On Vega colony?" Kirk yelled back. "I know that's what this is all about."

"Then you know it doesn't matter if I die. Not now. All that matters is the Varkolak get what's coming to them. What they've had coming to them since they destroyed Vega V, and my parents with it. I hate them, Kirk! I hate the Varkolak. But I hate the Federation even more. Why didn't they go to war then? Why did they make concessions? Back down? Damn it, Kirk—there's a Varkolak colony on Vega V now! How many Federation citizens have died at the hands of the Varkolak, and still the Federation won't fight!"

"We do fight. Every time. There were just as many Varkolak who died at Vega V as Federation people."

"Women and children? Mothers and fathers?"

"What about the Federation attack on Chi Herculis?" Kirk shot back. "Those weren't soldiers there. And what about you? You tried to kill the president of the United Federation of Planets!"

"No! No one died in that explosion! I made sure of it! It was carefully controlled. I wasn't *really* trying to kill her—just make sure everybody thought the Varkolak wanted her dead."

"And the bomb at the medical conference? People really did die there. *I* almost died."

"That bomb was set to go off in between sessions! That room was supposed to be clear! It's not my fault if people stayed around to talk."

"Are you listening to yourself, Nadja?"

"I thought you of all people would understand, Kirk," Nadja told him through the hiss of the coolant leak. "Wasn't your father killed by some alien ship?"

"Yeah," Kirk said. "Yeah, he was."

"I'll bet that made your childhood pretty wonderful, didn't it?" Nadja said.

Kirk looked away. Of course it hadn't. His childhood had been terrible. Awful. Of all people, he *did* know what it was like to lose a parent that young and to know that somewhere out there was the person responsible for it.

"All right, yeah," Kirk said. "It was the worst thing that ever happened to me and my mom and my brother. And yeah, I'd like to give whoever did it a bloody nose someday. But that doesn't mean I've spent my whole life trying to figure out a way to kill off their entire race."

"I have," Nadja said, and a cluster of bright red bolts of phaser fire came tearing through the cloud. Kirk hit the deck just in time to feel them scorch past and hit the doorway behind him, destroying it in an explosion of sparks and twisted duranium. Kirk put his hands over his head until she was finished shooting and had run away.

Ahead of him was a poisonous cloud that would eat him alive if he so much as touched it. Behind him was a mangled corridor he couldn't get through without a phaser. He was trapped.

Kirk thunked his head down on the metal floor and cursed himself. He'd forgotten that plasma coolant wouldn't stop phaser fire.

CH.29.30
Depressurization

Leonard McCoy was lost.

He stared at the mass of conduits and circuits and coils and who knew what else that made up the bomb Nadja had made, desperately trying to remember the few general engineering classes he'd been forced to take as a cadet. He'd done his best in those courses, but he had plenty enough to remember from his medical classes. The human brain was only capable of so much recall, damn it! How was he supposed to defuse a bomb an engineer—and a damn good one, at that—had jerry-rigged in Argos's Jefferies tube? There wasn't even a visible timer or blue and red wires. In the old holo-vids, bombs like this always had stuff like that, didn't they? But not this one. For all he knew, this damn thing was going to blow up in his face any second.

"Think, McCoy," he told himself. His eyes swept the machinery again, trying to make sense of it. "Think, damn it."

Was that a cryogenic fluid transfer there? Or a synthetic gravity-field bleed? Wow, doctors and engineers even used a different language.

Wait. They might use a different language, but the principles, the underlying mechanics, they were similar, weren't they? Ships, stations—they were living things, in their way. They had hearts (reactors) and minds (computer cores). They had eyes and ears (scanners and sensors) and other organs besides, like transporters and gravity generators. And feeding those systems, linking them, were the nerves and arteries of conduits and pipes.

And this bomb—it was a cancer. An anomalous growth that had attached itself to its host, using its own energy, its own resources, to kill it. All he had to do was remove the tumor, and the patient would survive.

Starships and bodies: The underlying subjects were the same. Only the terminology was different.

Sort of.

If McCoy wanted to survive, he was going to have to pretend they were, anyway. That, and a few half-remembered lectures on starship systems were the only chance they had.

McCoy pulled Nadja's abandoned tool kit to him and sifted through it, looking for a likely instrument. Finally he found something that reminded him of a laser scalpel and turned to the improvised bomb.

"Don't worry," he told the station. "This isn't going to hurt a bit. I hope."

Nyota Uhura was nervous.

Unlike Spock and his communication to the Federation fleet, she needed not only audio but video as well. Varkolak was a complicated language—far too complicated to be transmitted by audio only. Without a slight twitch of the tail and a raised snout, the verb "to retreat" sounded the same as the verb "to attack." She definitely didn't want to say one thing when she meant the other or have her meaning be ambiguous. This was too important.

But it was going to be hard enough to reproduce the Varkolak body movements accurately, particularly as she didn't have a tail—crass comments in the Warp Core not withstanding. But certainly there had to be some allowance for Varkolak who had lost their tails in accidents or in battle. She hoped a few good shakes of what tail she had would suffice.

"Federation transmission complete," Spock told her.

Uhura nodded. On the viewscreen, the Federation ships were deploying to counter the movements of the Varkolak fleet, but so far no one had fired.

It was now or never.

Uhura hit the transmit button and hailed the Varkolak ships in their own language.

No response. Not that she'd expected one.

"All right, I'm talking, whether you're listening or not," Uhura muttered.

She glanced back at Spock, who watched her intently. She felt a surge of self-consciousness under his gaze. She was about to wiggle and twitch and pose in what would appear to uneducated observers to be an embarrassingly silly, solitary dance without music. But the words of her high school Andorian language teacher came back to her again then, as they often did: *Great linguists are great because they aren't afraid to say the wrong thing and sound silly.*

Or look *silly*, Uhura silently amended.

"Varkolak Armada," she said in simple Varkolak, moving with the sounds. "I am U-hu-ra, of the Federation. A bad person/cur tricks the Federation. A bad person/cur tricks the Ones Who Remain Wild. The two groups/packs attack without reason/purpose. Contact/communication is wanted."

Uhura paused, trying to think how to proceed. How in the world did you say "call off the dogs" in Varkolak?

Pack-Howler Woolart was surprised.

The communications officer on the *Txakarra-Hartz*,

the flagship of the Varkolak Armada, couldn't believe his eyes and his ears. But there it was, as plain as the snout on his face. He turned and interrupted the barked orders and replies in the ship-den.

"Alpha-Captain GarrRka! We are receiving a transmission from the Federation telescope at the edge of the sector."

"Ignore it," GarrRka told him. "They only mean to distract us."

"Yes. But, sir—it is in Varkolak."

That seemed to get the alpha-captain's attention. The rest of the bridge's attention too.

"Is it Captain Lartal?" GarrRka asked. "One of the others?"

"No, sir. It is a Tail-less. A Terran, I think."

GarrRka's tail twitched with curiosity. "On screen," he said.

The forward viewscreen in the *Txakarra-Hartz*'s ship-den switched from the line of Starfleet ships ahead of them to a hairless, tail-less Terran female trying to speak Varkolak.

"Varkolak Armada," the ugly animal said. "I am U-hu-ra, of the Federation. A cur meddles the Federation. A cur meddles the Ones Who Remain Wilderness. . . ."

"She's mauling our language!" the helmsman said.

"Yes," GarrRka said, leaning forward on his bed. "But at least she's trying. And what she's *saying* is far more important. . . ."

● ⠂ ⋅ ✦ ⋅ ✦ ⋅ ● ⋅

Jim Kirk was too late.

The station's safety programs shut down the plasma coolant leak, but not in time for Kirk to catch Nadja before she reached the escape pods. Nadja was already inside one, prepping it for launch as Kirk careened into the small emergency shuttlebay. He hit the door controls to her pod, but they didn't respond. Nadja had locked him out. She saw him through the small window in the door and gave him an unhappy smile and a wave good-bye.

Kirk wasn't ready to say good-bye yet. "Come on, come on," he said, looking around the room for something to use to get inside that escape pod, but there was nothing.

A phaser would have come in really *handy right now*, Kirk told himself. He patted himself down in desperation, to see if he had anything useful on him, and his hand found something hard and metal in his pocket.

A titanium spork!

Kirk pulled it out and twirled it in his fingers triumphantly. "My kingdom for a spork!" he said. Inside the capsule, Nadja couldn't hear him. Or didn't care. She was tapping at the pod's navigation computer. Any second now she would jettison away from the station and be gone.

Kirk attacked the panel housing the door controls with the spork and pried it away. Inside was a mass of conduits and coils. He yanked some out from the wall, separated two wires from the rest, and used the sharp edge of the spork to cut through their plastic casings. Flipping the spork sideways, he touched it to the two exposed wires.

Crack!

Kirk jumped back as he got a jolt, but it worked: The hot-wired door hissed open. Nadja turned, surprised, and went for her phaser. Kirk dove in after her and slammed her back into the console. The phaser skittered away. Kirk grabbed Nadja's wrists, and they wrestled in the small space, unable to do much more than elbow and knee each other.

"Give up!" Kirk told her. "There's still time to make this right!"

"I'd . . . rather . . . die!" Nadja told him. She worked a hand free and mashed at the emergency launch override controls behind her.

Red lights flashed. "Warning," the computer said. "Rear escape-pod hatch is ajar."

Kirk looked down at Nadja, wide-eyed. "Don't," he told her.

"Computer, override safeties," Nadja said. "Launch escape pod!"

Kirk had just enough time to throw himself at the station before the escape pod exploded away underneath them. With one hand he grabbed a handrail just inside the door. With the other, he held on tight to Nadja, keeping her from being sucked out into space with the pod as all the air in the room rushed out.

Kirk's Starfleet space survival training kicked in. He had about fifteen seconds if he did everything right. He breathed out the air in his lungs so the quick depressurization wouldn't expand and force air into his blood, but that meant he had even less time before he blacked out. He would take the trade. Kirk could already feel the saliva in his mouth heating up as the superquick reduction in air pressure lowered the boiling point of his bodily fluids below his body temperature, but the depressurization had one benefit, at least. Now that all the air was replaced with vacuum, it made hauling himself and Nadja back inside easier. He dragged the already unconscious Nadja back over the sill, then pulled himself up over the handrail, and touched the spork to the exposed leads in the door panel.

With a silent spark and a jolt Kirk could barely feel, the door slammed shut. He slumped to the floor, and the emergency systems repressurized the room, flooding it with breathable air again. Sweet, glorious air.

Kirk wasn't sure how long his communicator had been chirping at him when he finally realized it and worked it out of his pocket. His fingers were swollen and bruised from the blood vessels that had burst just under his skin, and as feeling returned to him, he knew he must be black and blue all over.

He flipped his communicator open and listened, too tired to even say hello.

"Jim! Jim, it's me," said Bones. "I did it! I defused the bomb! Did you get Nadja?"

Kirk nodded, then realized Bones couldn't hear that. "Yeah," he whispered.

"Jim? Are you all right?"

"No," he said. "Escape pods. Vacuum."

"I'll be right there," Bones said.

Kirk let his arm drop. *You do that*, he thought. He turned to look at the bruised and unconscious Nadja Luther and realized he still had the spork in his other hand. He flopped an arm over onto Nadja and touched her with it.

"Tag," he told her. "I win."

CH.30.30
Mating Season

"Sit down," Admiral Barnett told them, and Spock and Uhura sat down.

"Admiral, before you begin, I'd just like to apologize for my part in giving the Varkolak sniffer to Nadja Luther," Uhura said. "I take full responsibility, and I'm prepared to tender my resignation from the Academy."

Admiral Barnett waved her confession away. "You were acting as an agent of the Federation, Cadet. Besides, you had no way of knowing the Varkolak device would be used for anything like that."

"As I have told you," Spock said to her. "In addition to the fact that you almost single-handedly averted an interplanetary war."

"Yes," Barnett said. "There's that too. Damn good work, Cadet. Both of you. You've made the Academy look very good today. Very good, indeed. You'll both be receiving commendations on your records."

"Thank you, sir," said Spock.

"What about Nadja Luther?" Uhura asked.

Barnett frowned. "Not such a good day for the Academy. But rest assured that she'll go to prison for a long time for her crimes."

"And what of the Graviton Society?" Spock asked.

Barnett restacked the PADDs on his desk. "It's being looked into."

Uhura and Spock exchanged doubtful glances.

"With all due respect, sir," Uhura said, "but it's been 'looked into.' That's what Spock and I were *doing*."

"There is a clear and present danger, Admiral," said Spock. "Left unchecked, the Graviton Society might grow into something far more dangerous. Nadja Luther is a disturbing case in point."

"Nadja Luther was a rogue agent. You've said so yourself in your report," Barnett said.

"Admiral—" Uhura began.

Barnett held up a hand. "You are hereby under orders not to mention the Graviton Society or to pursue this matter any further. Either of you. Is that understood?"

Uhura couldn't believe what she was hearing. She looked to Spock. One of his eyebrows was raised higher than she ever thought it possible for an eyebrow to rise.

"I was asked to investigate the Graviton Society at Captain Pike's request," Spock told Barnett.

"And I'm an admiral, and I'm telling you to drop it," Barnett replied. He leaned forward conspiratorially. "Damn it. Do you two realize how many current Starfleet officers were members of the Graviton Society when they were cadets? Still *are* members?"

"Were *you* a member, Admiral?" Uhura asked.

"You're out of line, Cadet." He leaned back in his chair. "You have your orders. Both of you. Dismissed."

Uhura began to stand, but Spock stayed in his seat.

"I am afraid I am unable to comply, Admiral," Spock said.

Uhura couldn't believe what she was hearing. Apparently neither could the admiral. He blinked in confusion, like Spock had just confessed to being an undercover Romulan.

"Are you—are you disobeying a direct order, Commander?" he asked finally.

"No, sir. Or rather, I disobeyed it before it was given. I cannot go back in time and alter history; thus, I am unable now to comply."

Barnett frowned, trying to understand what Spock was telling him. "You mean . . . you've already done something? About the society?"

"Yes, sir. I communicated the group's existence and complicity in this matter to the Federation News Service. Along with the names of everyone we discovered were members of the Graviton Society. I believe the news is already circulating on the feeds."

Barnett was apoplectic. "No one gave you an order to release that information, Commander!"

"And no one gave me an order not to. Until now. My apologies."

Uhura almost laughed at Spock's half-hearted apology, but she knew it would only make things worse.

"Out," Barnett told them. "Just . . . get out."

This time they both left as quickly as they could. When they were finally outside in the bright sunshine of the California afternoon, Uhura took Spock's arm in hers.

"That was pretty devious, Spock."

"I suspected our discoveries might be covered up at some point, so I took prohibitive action. The only thing that can erase a shadow is light."

Uhura laughed. "Remind me never to get on your bad side, Spock."

"Nyota, never get on my bad side."

Uhura brought them to a stop. "Spock, was that a joke?"

"A small one. Yes."

Uhura smiled. Maybe there was hope for them yet.

• · ·✦ ·. ✦ · ✦ ·. .

Proximity alerts went off and red lights flashed as Sulu steered the USS *Yorktown* between two shuttle-sized asteroids. He winced as one of them glanced off the underside of the ship, jolting them, but he quickly forgot about it as phaser blasts from the pursuing Romulan scout ships rocked them harder.

"Shields down to fifty-one percent!" Chekov cried from the seat beside Sulu at the conn.

"Return fire!" Tikhonov yelled from the captain's chair. "Full power to aft shields!"

"Aye, aye, aye," Chekov muttered. "If the phasers don't get us, the asteroids will."

"I'm not going to let that happen," Sulu told him, swinging the *Yorktown* out of the way of a space station–sized asteroid.

"Stay away from the big ones!" Tikhonov cried.

"Yeah, thanks for the advice," Sulu whispered.

A series of phaser blasts knocked them around, and a part of Sulu's console sparked. He waved the smoke away and tapped at it, a pit of dread forming in his stomach.

"We've lost impulse engines!" he announced. "Thrusters only!"

"We're dead," Tikhonov said.

"No," said Sulu. He pointed to an enormous asteroid on the viewscreen. "Chekov, what's the mass of that asteroid? The big one there?"

"Its mass?" Chekov tapped at his sensor readout. "Four times ten to the sixteenth kilograms. I suggest we not run into it."

"I'm not planning to," Sulu said, but his actions proved otherwise. He heard Chekov gasp beside him as he used the *Yorktown*'s existing impulse inertia and the ship's thrusters to aim straight for it, ignoring the smaller asteroids that banged off the shields and hull on the way.

"No, no!" Tikhonov cried. "I said stay *away* from the big ones!"

"We're going to turn," Sulu announced. "You might want to put all energy to the port shields."

"I—" Tikhonov said, ready to argue, but as the asteroid loomed large in front of them, Sulu hit the forward starboard thrusters and the aft port thrusters hard, swinging the back end of the *Yorktown* around the orbit of the asteroid, like a car losing its back wheels on wet pavement. The asteroid stayed in front of them the whole time as they swung around it, but their port side was exposed to the still-attacking Romulan ships.

"Energy to port shields, aye!" Chekov said.

The Romulan ships peppered them with phaser shots, but soon they were behind the moon-sized asteroid, and Sulu hit the forward thrusters, pushing them backward away from the asteroid—and backward out of the asteroid belt.

"You used the asteroid's gravity to propel us out!" Chekov cried.

It had worked, but Sulu knew they weren't out of

the woods yet. On the viewscreen ahead of them, the Romulan scout ships dipped under and around the giant asteroid and came straight at them.

"Go to warp! Go to warp!" Tikhonov said.

Sulu was already laying in the coordinates. As soon as the *Yorktown's* nose went below the outer edge of the asteroid field, he punched it, the starfield in front of them streaking away to a blur.

The viewscreen went black, and the red-alert sirens stopped as the simulation ended and the lights came up. The sim crew breathed its usual sigh of relief, and Tikhonov celebrated.

"We did it!"

Chekov turned to shake Sulu's hand.

"Fantastic!" Chekov said.

Sulu grinned. "Thanks."

The door to the observation room opened, and an Academy instructor came in the room. "Nice job," she said. "Particularly there at the end."

"It was a simple matter of physics," Tikhonov said. "I knew that if we—"

"Actually, that was my idea," Sulu said, speaking up. "We didn't have impulse engines anymore, but we still had the forward momentum. All we needed was a little help from our big friend there. We didn't have time to talk about it, so I just did it."

"Nice job, Mr."—the commander checked her PADD—"Sulu. And well done, everyone. You're dismissed."

Tikhonov wasn't thrilled about Sulu taking the credit for the maneuver, he could tell, but he was happy to tell everyone about all the other brilliant decisions he'd made as he escorted them out. At the lockers outside, Chekov congratulated Sulu again—this time for not letting Tikhonov hog all the credit.

"Well," Chekov said. "Good-bye until next class, then."

"Pavel, wait," Sulu said, catching the young cadet before he was gone. "Did you hear about this Assassination Game, where cadets run around trying to 'kill' one another with sporks from the cafeteria?"

"Aye," Chekov said. "But it is over. The admiral made them stop."

Sulu put his arm around Chekov's shoulder. "He made *them* stop. But not us. What do you say we start our own?"

"I say, we can do this! But are you sure? You are always saying you do not have the time for such things."

"Plans change," Sulu said. "Now, what do you think about water pistols as weapons . . . ?"

Kirk and Bones got some strange looks on the trolley. Perhaps not surprisingly, they had one whole side of it to themselves, too.

Kirk was sure it had nothing to do with the Varkolak sitting between them.

Lartal's tongue lolled out the side of his mouth as the streetcar rattled up and down San Francisco's hills, and Kirk suddenly had visions of a dog hanging its head out the window of a car, tail wagging, tongue flapping in the wind. He smiled to himself, then tried his best to put the thought away. Very, very far away.

The streetcar came to a stop outside the Dragon Gate, and the conductor announced the stop: Chinatown.

"This is us," Kirk told them.

"You think she is *here*?" Lartal asked Kirk when they were out on the sidewalk.

"Look. I started to think about it," Kirk told him. "You triangulated her position. You know she's inside a twenty-five-square-block radius. But that's a lot of ground to cover, especially since you . . ." Kirk looked for a polite way to put it.

"Were recently public enemy number one," Bones filled in.

"Thanks, Bones."

Bones shrugged, as if to say, *Well? Am I wrong?*

"So, you can't just go roaming around the city again, or you might cause a riot. But I got to thinking, the way you track is by sense of smell, isn't it?"

"Mostly," Lartal said.

"So once your mate picked a planet to hide on, she would choose some place crowded to lay low, where she'd be hard to find. *And*," Kirk said, waving a hand at the Dragon Gate, "some place with lots of new smells to mask her scent."

Lartal sniffed at the air with his snout. Even from here, Kirk could smell roast duck and incense, bundled herbs and rotting vegetables, baking fortune cookies, ramen and dim sum.

"Yes!" Lartal said, taking off at a run. "She is here!"

"Whoa! Hey!" Kirk called, but Lartal wouldn't be stopped. Instead, Kirk and Bones ran with him as best they could as he followed his nose through the neighborhood. He would stop to sniff at a lamppost or a fire hydrant, then be off again just as quickly, following a scent.

"For crying out loud," Bones said as he pulled up panting alongside Kirk on one of their frequent stops. "The only thing I can smell anymore is the garbage."

Kirk had to agree. Chinatown might be full of wonderous sights and smells, but it was equally full of disgusting ones. And it didn't help that it was apparently trash collection day.

Lartal's nose led them to Portsmouth Square, the big public park in the heart of Chinatown. The place was full of people of all races and species. A group of Andorians practiced *ushaan-to* beside Chinese San Franciscans doing tai chi. Some Rigelians played Frisbee, and an aged Vulcan and a human child played three-dimensional chess.

Lartal slid off into the trees.

"Wait a minute, what's he—" Bones started to say, but Kirk shushed him, pointing.

Sitting on a bench beneath the statue of the Goddess of Democracy was someone in a dark brown cloak that covered her face.

And most of her tail.

She sat on the bench reading a PADD as Lartal stalked closer. Before either Kirk or Bones could gasp, she was up and running, Lartal at her heels. But she wasn't running the way you ran when you wanted to get away from somebody; she was running the way you did when you were playing with them, leading them on a chase. She wove in and out of souvenir stalls and food carts, jumped benches and retaining walls, scattered bocce players and jugglers.

Lartal finally caught up with her in the middle of a grassy lawn, bowling her over and nipping at her, like two dogs at play. Kirk and Bones ran up to where they lay, still pawing and wrestling with each other, and Kirk suddenly got the feeling he was intruding on something private.

"Bones, wait," Kirk said. "Maybe we should just, you know . . ." He nodded away from them.

"Wait!" Lartal said, laughing. "Kirk, meet my mate, Gren."

The two Varkolak got up from the ground and tried to make themselves presentable. When her cloak was shed, Kirk saw that Gren's fur was a startling white with gray-brown patches, almost a complement to Lartal's patterning. Her face was thinner and longer, her tail bushier and shorter, and, though it seemed strange for Kirk to think it, she was altogether rather beautiful.

"Charmed, I'm sure," Gren said, giving Kirk her paw.

"My friend Bones," Kirk said. Gren's eyes grew wide at the word.

"Leonard McCoy," Bones told her. "Nice to meet you."

Lartal and Gren nipped and nuzzled each other, and Kirk definitely began to feel like he and Bones were a third nacelle.

"So, we'll just leave you alone so you can have some privacy, then," Kirk said, realizing that there was little privacy to be had in the middle of Portsmouth Square. "Although, you might want to try those trees over there . . ."

Lartal laughed. "The trees, Kirk?"

Kirk groaned. If Lartal and his mate did what he thought they were about to do, it would be an interplanetary incident all over again.

"Come on, Lartal," Gren told him. "I have a room at the Huntington."

"The Huntington?" Kirk asked. That was one of the

oldest, fanciest hotels in San Francisco.

"What did you think, Kirk?" said Lartal. "We're not animals."

"Well, Bones," Kirk said after they'd left Lartal and his mate. "This is one for our memoirs."

"Yeah," McCoy said. "I think I'll call this chapter 'Heartbreak at Cavallo Point.'"

"Still torn up about Nadja, Bones? Don't be. She wasn't the right girl for you. You know how I could tell?"

"No."

"She stole your access code, tried to frame you for attempted murder, and then shot you."

"Thanks," McCoy told him. "I'll watch out for that in the future. In fact, I'll lead with that next time. 'Say, you don't happen to be interested in me only because I have Level Two med-lab clearance and I'm a sucker for a pretty face, do you?'"

"Aw, come on, Bones. You just need to find the right girl. As a matter of fact, me and Braxxy and a couple of the guys were thinking about hitting the Warp Core tonight. . . ."

"Oh no," McCoy said. "I'm done with women for the foreseeable future. As in the next century."

They hopped a streetcar for Golden Gate and made

their way to a pair of empty seats at the back.

"Got your lab work to keep you warm, is that it?" Kirk said.

"I'll manage," McCoy replied. "A lot better without women than with."

They sat down and found themselves staring into the eyes of the most beautiful girl Leonard McCoy had ever seen. She was curvy and petite, with short black hair the color of licorice and eyes the color of a New Orleans morning.

"Hey," Kirk said to the girl. "Aren't you in my Interspecies Protocol class?"

She smiled, her dimples forming little quasars of cute in her cheeks. "Yeah. I'm Amy Westin."

"Jim Kirk. This here's Leonard McCoy. Say hello, Leonard."

"Huh? What?" McCoy said. He hadn't been listening.

He was head over heels in love.